Artwork and photography by author.

Other Books by Zach S.Z. Murphy:

Cathedral of the Damned

Aberrations

Thousand-Year Dream

Revolution. Progression. Mastery.

Thousand-Year Dream: Vilkacis

Know your Enemy.

Know Yourself.

Know when to Strike.

WARBORN

Chapter 1

*W*ith the eerie morning light creeping into the dying night, the two samurai, Kyamoto and Tamashii, unsheathed their katanas and clashed violently. At first, they passed through one another like ghosts, parrying and avoiding each move. The leaves of the garden around them rattled from their mortal dance, blades clacking sharply and disturbing the birds from the trees.

Quietly, both stepped back and circled each other – Kyamoto with a sly smirk, and Tamashii with a deep frown. It was the end of the nineteenth century, and Japan was modernizing at a feverish rate. Traditions were kept in the homes and temples, and matters of honor left to the lawyers, but in this feud, the desire to let blood flow was rooted deep in the past. In the privacy of the garden overflowing with flora and trees, witnessed by a handful who respected the old ways, the two men stopped circling each other and met blades again.

Kyamoto struck hard, transitioned to a feint, then slashed horizontally across Tamashii's left elbow. In the same space, Tamashii delivered a mirror counterattack and sliced across Kyamoto's left elbow. Both reflexively shied back, their sleeves ripped and soaking crimson, and despite the pain, they recovered their stance and attacked.

Tamashii belted his opponent's left knee, and Kyamoto, while stumbling past him, brought his edge neatly across Tamashii's waist. Blood spilled on their kimonos and on the grass, but they continued the assaults. Pieces of delicate branches and flowers from plants and blooming trees around them tumbled to the ground from their swings, until Tamashii cut Kyamoto's right shoulder. Growling angrily, Kyamoto retreated in a gambit to draw his opponent to him and drove his blade through Tamashii's right leg.

Tamashii yelped and limped away quickly before Kyamoto could thrust again. He let out a determined sigh, glaring at his foe.

Wordlessly, both men sprinted towards each other, raising their swords in a final strike. Both collided violently – Kyamoto's ear rolled across the grass, and half of Tamashii's blade impaling its tip on a maple tree's bark.

At the same distance away from each other as they had been when they first started, the two samurai turned and faced one another. The right side of Kyamoto's face, from forehead to jaw, was splayed open and bleeding, while Tamashii held his chest tightly from an irreparable wound to his heart and lungs.

After a moment of heavy breathing, both looked at each other in the eye and bowed formally. In this final act, Tamashii dropped the broken half of his katana, fell on his knees, then on his face – dead. Kyamoto, in terrible pain from his wounds, straightened up from his bow. He regarded the fallen samurai with a grudging sense of respect, then crumpled to the ground in final rest....

The tremors of a distant mortar explosion shook the ground, and the sharpened tip of a pencil accidentally tore a gash across the page of a leather-bound journal, interrupting the old tale from a faraway land. Nor dream nor memory.

With his back against the wall inside a deep dugout, carved out of necessity with shovels and pickaxes, and shored up by wooden beams and boards, Brazen calmly set down the pencil and leaned his head back. His fierce dark eyes, the color of roasted maple, with hair to match, glanced up at the dust and bits of debris tumbling from the ceiling of the shelter; the tallow lamps rattling with the violent vibrations. Around him, tired British Commonwealth soldiers and officers tried to rest as the stalemate trench battle with the German line continued for yet another night. It was a battle of attrition devised by armchair commanders too slow to adapt to new technologies and tactics, churning one battle after another into faceless conflicts between guns and numbers that yielded great losses for little gain.

It was the start of 1916, in the Western trenches deep within France's old borders, and the end of the war was nowhere in sight.

He spotted an Army courier sifting past a group of wounded men returning from the infirmary, his uniform splattered with mud from his trek through the communication trenches. Brazen closed his journal, using the pencil as a bookmark, and placed it into his bag as the courier approached.

"Beg your pardon, Sergeant," the courier greeted, "I was sent to deliver you a message from the War Office." He leaned closer and momentarily broke away from the uppity undertone of his voice. "The Gauntlet has dropped."

Brazen quietly acknowledged the message, knowing exactly what the cryptic words meant.

The Army courier tipped his hat in courtesy. "Sir."

With letters and packages to deliver in haste, the courier left to his other duties. Brazen gathered his Lee Enfield Mk. III bolt-action rifle and gear, pausing for a moment to admire the sheathed katana with an ornate scabbard that he inherited from the kind old woman who adopted him after his mother had passed away. It felt like so long ago, but it was a cornerstone of his adult life now. Brazen respectfully pulled out the blade, several inches of its tip broken off, and still incredibly sharp.

Like his rifle and shovel, the sword was a stark reminder of what it took to survive amidst the carnage, and what he fought for. He slid the blade back into the scabbard, solidly secured, and lovingly passed his fingers on the lacquered surface, before hooking it away within a hidden loop in his backpack. Not the standard equipment issued to soldiers, but for his area of expertise, he was given the exception.

He gave an appreciating nod to his fellow compatriots resting in their holed-out spots along the muddy wall as they waterproofed their boots, offering them what was left of his daily rations – some canned corn beef and hard biscuits. They saluted him, and wished him well as Brazen left the perceived safety of the dugout and into the reserve trench.

Holding the thick canvas carrying strap of his bolt-action rifle over his shoulder, Brazen maneuvered past the staggered shifts of soldiers coming from the exhaustive frontline fire bays. He kept steady on the wooden slats laid down on the ground to keep soldiers' feet reasonably dry on his approach to the support trench, as gunfire and mortars were sporadically traded between armies. British, Scottish, and Canadian infantrymen crowded the muddy channels, some firing at encroaching enemy observers on behest of their officers, while others laid within makeshift canopies and funk holes resting beside the dead and wounded waiting to be carried off to the field hospital not far from the city of Verdun, though it was essentially a bombed-out church used as a casualty clearing station. Spent bullet casings and mortar shrapnel littered the ground. Boxes filled with spare ammunition and spare gun parts also coveted the few feet of available space between grimy earth and uniformed bodies, creating obstacles that slowed down any quick march.

With a section of the communication trench being repaired after a shell had buckled it earlier, Brazen sought another route that took him close the main line of resistance. A Canadian Division Officer suddenly rose up to spur his squad to charge onto the battlefield, and the men valiantly climbed over the wall of the zigged-zagged trench onto incoming German fire. Their courageous shouting was easily overcome by machinegun fire, and within the space of a heartbeat, one of the first soldiers to commit to the fray was killed instantly. Barely out of the ditch, the dead infantryman tumbled backward, and rolled into the dirt directly in Brazen's path.

The deafening cacophony of fierce warfare, and the rife stench of putrid mud, human filth, gunpowder, and smoke was almost unbearable, but Brazen weathered it with tight resolve.

Maintaining indifference, he stepped over the dead soldier, and continued to the officers' tightly tucked headquarters up ahead.

Briskly saluting the two nervous British troopers assigned as guards for the day, Brazen opened the door to the headquarters and stepped in.

The confined grotto was occupied with liaisons sifting crucial information on telephones and telegrams, while diligent officers discussed tactics and fresh intel over maps spread out on uneven wooden tables. The headquarters also served as storage for food rations and just about everything else, but Brazen was interested only in one officer who was keeping to himself in an improvised anteroom where the cots and beddings were kept as luxuries for the high-ranking brass.

Captain Reginald Goodwin, sporting a neat moustache, meticulously-combed dark hair, and a slim-fitting uniform washed free of bloodstains, dirt, and piss, sat by a small worktable, under a lantern that swung too easily with every tremor resounding from the mortar blasts. With careful devotion, a dusty magnifying glass, and lots of patience, he worked on the delicate inner gears of an antique mantle clock. While his Webley Mk VI officer's revolver was holstered at his side, an American-made Colt M1911 was close at hand on the tabletop. The self-loading pistol was not all that unusual except that it was finely engraved along its receiver, barrel, and slide with flourishing, leafy vines, and the name *'Elowen'* in cursive script.

Brazen saluted formally to the captain. "Sir."

Goodwin was focused on his watchmaker's delicate task, talking softly to himself. "...One peg moves the gear... the gear moves the hand... and the hand moves time. Did you know I found this old thing discarded by the wayside when we landed? Damn shame not to give this timepiece a second chance at a good life."

"Captain?"

"My grandfather opened up a shop in York selling clocks; in little time he repaired them, and then he was building them from scratch." Too focused on adjusting the clock's regulators, Goodwin lost himself in recollection, though he was aware he was with company. "The appreciation of the craft skipped a generation, of course. My father was only interested in money – or lack thereof. I was the lucky one, I suppose."

Winding the internal mechanism, the gears turned, and Goodwin felt a humble sense of victory. "Do you know the two things that I greatly appreciate about watchmaking?"

"Patience and precision," Brazen answered.

A nearby explosion rocked the table and tools, unsettling the mantle clock to a sudden stop.

Goodwin's expression soured. "Two things sorely lacking in this war."

"Captain Goodwin, sir," Brazen addressed with far more patience held in reserve, "may I have a word with you?"

Goodwin briefly glanced up from his chore, recognizing the man at last. "Orin, my good lad, what brings you out of the muck and mire?"

"This communiqué from the War Office."

Brazen produced the letter he was given, and laid it on the table. Intrigued, the captain gingerly set down the clock and his tools, noticing that Brazen was eying the Colt. "It was a parting gift from my wife, which she purchased with my own money. It's a good reminder, as a well as a warning should I mingle with the local women and become fluent in their funny accent."

Brazen understood that a woman's love and scorn was nothing to trifle with. "Respect the weapon, as you would a woman."

"Properly stated, Sergeant." Goodwin opened the letter, and read it thoroughly, becoming terrifyingly perplexed by its message.

He looked up at Brazen. "Sergeant, please close the door."

Brazen complied, and closed the small, creaky door shut.

"This order comes directly from the Secret Service Bureau, signed by the big "C" himself. Are you part of Military Intelligence?"

"I'm not at liberty to confirm that, sir," Brazen replied. "All I can divulge is that those orders require you to temporarily dismiss me from my current station. Discreetly."

"Discreetly?" Goodwin repeated, still aghast by the severity of the secret orders. "That's somewhat of an understatement considering the circumstances."

As if to accentuate his retort, another nearby explosion rattled the headquarters.

Brazen was unfazed. "I will also require a uniform from one of the German prisoners we captured yesterday... sir."

"If you plan to cross the enemy line," Goodwin warned, "it better be for good reason. You've been one of my best ever since you waltzed in from the Legion of Frontiersmen. In fact, I've been impressing you on the letters I send to my wife... I'd hate to end it with a tragic note."

Brazen appreciated the compliment from his captain, but there was little time to press on trivialities. "I will also need you to assign me to one of the night raiding parties."

Goodwin laughed at Brazen's cold, but professional demeanor. He folded the letter back in its envelope, set it up near the flaming hot lantern until the edges caught fire, and threw it down on the ground. He picked up the clock off the tabletop, as the letter burned to flaky embers.

"By your leave, Sergeant. Do what you have to do for crown and country, and I'll handle the paperwork."

Brazen saluted. "Thank you, Captain."

"Godspeed." Goodwin watched Brazen leave, wondering if he'll ever see him again, then returned his attention to the clock, hoping to get it working before the war demanded his time.

Chapter 2

*W*earing coats and quilts darkened with dirt and wax to shield them from the unexpected dangers under the moonless sky, the volunteer Highland regiment soldiers of the night raiding party hunched low as they crossed the cratered terrain toward the German line. They passed broken trees, stagnant puddles, and the bodies of the fallen, both men and horses, deprived of a decent burial by the lack of a sustainable ceasefire. They carefully slipped through row upon row of tangled barbed-wire meant to deter any forward charge, clipping open a small path with wire cutters, and wary of any traps laid by both sides of the conflict.

Tagging along several paces from the nervous soldiers was Brazen, his coat clasped tightly to conceal his scrounged German uniform. He kept focused, counting under his breath the time lapsing between the Germans' ubiquitous red flares.

A flare shot up, and washed the ground in crimson light. Everyone crouched and stayed still, the leading raiding officer quietly berating those lagging behind. They waited as the visible German troopers scanned the area with their binoculars and sound locators – whose gramophone-style horns were mainly designed to track aircraft.

As the red flare sputtered and faded back into the murk, the soldiers moved again, this time with certain haste. They covered several yards before the next flare lit up the devastated field. Once again, everyone paused, keeping a low profile from unfriendly eyes.

The crimson light fizzled, returning the darkness, and the soldiers readied to hustle the last length of ground to the nearest of the entrenched fire bays, but Brazen instinctively remained still. He crouched lower, nearly prone, and peered around the German perimeter while holding back the impulse to follow the others.

Nearby, a crust-ridden Ross rifle sat amongst the dead, coveted by a Canadian infantryman who had lost his life to a foolish frontal charge the day before, and Brazen slowly reached out to take it. The weapon was excellent at long-range, but had a fundamental defect to its straight-pull bolt design that caused it to burr. He wiped the dirt and dried blood off the trigger and bolt components, then cruelly cocked it back to remove its jammed bullet casing. Yet another flare sprung up, and Brazen paused his movements, but used the spare scarlet light to check the hollow of the barrel and charge.

When the gloom returned to the field, he used the hem of his coat to clean out the tip of the muzzle. He then reached into his equipment belt for a small scope and a pocket-knife. Calmly, he screwed the scope onto the rifle mount behind the bolt mechanism. Taking a fresh bullet from his pouch, he cocked it in place.

He rested on a knee and brought the rifle to bear in an area of the enemy line roughly forty-five degrees from the advancing raiding party. He waited motionless until another flare enflamed the ground, only this time the Scottish soldiers were detected by the Germans.

A powerful gunshot rang out from a German sniper on an elevated area of the trench, hidden by wooden stakes and shredded coverings, and struck one of the trailing soldiers of the raiding party with a killing blow. The other German troops, now riled up and shouting, drew their attention and guns to the daring Scots who responded with a full suicidal dash into the enemy furrow.

Aided by the distraction and consternation, Brazen fired and killed the German sniper, then unscrewed the scope and tossed the Ross rifle aside. Heavy gunfire filled the air now, as the entire German trench descended on the raiding party. One by one the Scots fell to the hail of bullets, and though the brave soldiers scored a few kills themselves, they were no match against a determined defensive barrage and a slew of enemy stick grenades.

Still unseen, Brazen rushed quickly away from the hopeless fight, understanding time was whittling away. He removed his coat and Brodie steel helmet, leaving them behind as he approached the German trench.

With the enemy's attention drawn away, he descended unmolested into the gap behind a group of troopers eager to join the slaughter, but unwilling to leave their posts.

Brazen saw one of the soldiers' stahlhelm helmets beside some gear, casually picked one up and walked along without breaking his stride. His uniform completed, he melded with his surroundings, and snuck through the winding wood and concrete-laden labyrinth to the quartermaster's hole.

* * *

The unit officer, Franz Lieder, was alone in the lantern-lit confines of the raggedy, sandbagged depot. He counted the rations left in a crate, one of many stacked along the craggy wall, as part of his report to the commanding officer after an interruption in the supply lines, preferring to be in the hole killing rats than out in the cold, stinking mud waiting for a bomb to drop on his head.

The heavy canvas that covered the entrance gently furled, and Brazen stepped inside. With silent catlike grace, he approached the German officer, until the light from a lantern directly above him scattered some shadows.

Franz, immediately sensing the threat, spun around quickly and drew the Mauser C/96 pistol from his holster. Brazen moved faster, yanking the pistol from the officer's startled grip, and grappling the man's throat tightly with his thumb pressing into his Adam's apple.

[You are Franz Lieder?] Brazen asked in fluent Bavarian.

Franz tried to pull back, but Brazen's grip on his throat was unbreakable. His resistance further shirked as his own pistol was pressed against his cheek.

[You're an operative,] Brazen urged on. [You are known to the S-I-S.]

Franz, his voice coarse from Brazen's grip, seemed almost relieved. [You are a friend of Melville?]

Brazen relaxed his fingers, allowing Franz to gasp for breath, and slowly stepped back while keeping the Mauser aimed. [You were given a mission. You failed.]

[I did not fail,] Franz defended, rubbing the discomfort from his pained neck muscles. [I revealed to your superiors that the Kaiser commissioned an armament factory to begin mass-producing tanks based on the blueprints of the original successful prototype. Plans that were stolen from the War Office by one of your own.]

"Sigmund Tantalus." Brazen knew traitor by name through the subtle bits of information he had decrypted from the letter he had received, as well as his debrief before joining Captain Goodwin's rank and file on the Western Front. [You know of his whereabouts?]

[I know nothing else of use.]

Brazen doubted that statement. [You ceased your reports to the S-I-S a year ago; they believe you know where Tantalus' hiding, as well as the location of the factory.]

Franz Lieder sized up Brazen, regaining some confidence despite the Mauser pointed at him. [What will you do, kill me? They will hear the gunshot.]

[I don't a need gun to kill you,] Brazen replied icily.

To Franz's surprise, Brazen removed the bullet cartridge from the pistol and tossed both on the ground. Unexpectedly, a patrolman unknowingly interrupted the interrogation – abruptly pausing in mid-gibberish of replenishing his ammunition supplies. Thinking quickly, he pulled out his trench club with the intent of thrashing its eight-pointed cast-iron ring on Brazen's head.

Brazen reacted with lightning-fast reflexes, unsheathing the push dagger from his belt, and grabbing the soldier by the back of his collar. He tossed him against a pile of grain sacks, and repeatedly thrusted the perpendicular blade into the patrol's torso. Brazen's viciousness was surgical, striking the soldier with equally lethal blows until the patrolman collapsed.

Blood trickled down the push dagger, and stained Brazen's glove and sleeve, but paid no heed as he coolly turned to the double-agent.

[I... I don't know where the traitor is,] Franz said, stunned and submissive, [but I suspect he'll be at the factory. He won't be alone though.]

Brazen picked up the trench club and secured it to his equipment belt, keeping the bloody push dagger ready.

"Who's in command of this operation?"

"It was given to the Landsturm..." Franz replied in broken English, thrown off by the purposeful linguistic switch. "To oversee the factory with full disclosure."

"Location?"

Uncertain, Franz jostled his memory out of dire self-preservation. [Head east, near the farmlands around Stuttgart. You'll know for certain when it's guarded by a zeppelin, and a squadron of Fokkers.] He took pride of his spycraft, enticed by the monetary gain that far surpassed his meager paygrade, but looking at the dead soldier, his manipulative skills had limits. [How am I supposed to explain this?]

"You're clever; you've worked both sides of the fence. You caught him stealing supplies, he attacked, and you fought back. It was either him or you."

Without warning, Brazen slugged Franz across the head with the wrap-around metal handle of his push dagger. The German dropped fast and hard against the rations he had been counting moments before, and remained still.

Wiping the blood off the blade and onto his tunic's sleeve, Brazen sheathed the dagger, and picked up the Mauser and adjoining cartridge. Tucking it behind him, he promptly took his leave, when the night sky erupted in fiery hues as the German artillery pounded the opposing trenches.

The bulky, but effective howitzers, with its steel 'shoes' attached to the wheels, bombarded the protective dugouts nearly eight-thousand meters away. While a larger and heavier cannon, perched on a rail car with tracks for limited positioning, methodically discharged its payload – smashing mammoth craters on the battlefield.

Pressing against the trench avenue wall near ammunition cases, Brazen noted that the large cannon was manned by at least three gunners, and an artillery commander directed the bombardment. They were all deafened by the bone-rattling cacophony, and with the bulk of the forces arrayed up front to enjoy the terrifying spectacle or to brace for reprisal, the rear of the German camp was confidently complacent with its security.

Brazen inspected the cases beside him, and found a short supply of Eierhandgranate, or egg grenades, and picked up three. Climbing over the trench toward the artillery line, he kept his helmet low as he approached the rail car. With the backs of the gunners facing him, he set the three grenades and tossed them beneath the rail car.

He continued walking toward the small cavalry shack where the few live horses were kept, his stride quick but steady, and in five steps the egg grenades set off. The rail car ripped apart in the explosion, severing the cannon turret, and prematurely detonating its payload. The gunners were eviscerated in the blast, kicking up dirt and debris, and all else around the flash-point turned over from the shockwave.

Brazen timely dropped prone to the ground and covered his head as the explosion passed over him. In the bewilderment that followed, he quietly exited from the German side of the battlefield, freeing all the horses, while stealing the healthiest steed for himself, and disappearing into the surrounding thicket before the light of the flames reached him.

Chapter 3

Welders worked feverishly on the riveted steel hull of the mysterious monstrosity that engulfed a large area of the armament factory confines. Girders, catwalks, and chains surrounded them, and they were constantly watched by the jackbooted Landsturm provost guards.

Overseeing the construction on the highest catwalk was Sigmund Tantalus, who tussled nervously at his unkempt greying, golden hair while studying the calculations scribbled on a stack of worn papers that have been crumpled and undone dozens of times.

He was in the odd company of a thin, yet proud tactician from the Deutches Heer General Staff, Ralf Guderian, and a small but slender Japanese woman in dark civilian attire, Junigatsu. While the former had a West Prussian aristocratic air about him, spun from a family of militarists, the latter hailed from Hokkaido as part of an obscure sect of the Imperial Japanese secret police that couldn't be confirmed, only suspected. If that wasn't enough to insinuate her lethality, she wore a three-piece suit and tie tailored to her form, allowing her freedom of movement, and inciting the sexism and prejudice of men to her full advantage. In brains and brawn, she was not to be underestimated.

In frustration, Tantalus slapped his stack of notes against the support railing lining the catwalk. "Change the foreman or kill him! He's not giving proper instructions to the workmen!"

In the midst of adjusting his officer's peaked cap, piped in scarlet with a scarlet band, Guderian looked over at the resident genius. "What is it now?"

Not caring for the officer's deep German accent, Tantalus waved furiously at the construction below. "They think they're building a damn boat!"

Guderian grinned to offer the British turncoat some assurance, but the gesture came off rather chillingly. "In keeping the production of this fighting vehicle secret, the workmen are under the impression they are constructing a tracked water container. We borrowed this duplicity from your countrymen."

Haughtily, Tantalus walked off the catwalk and descended down the grated stairwell. Junigatsu wordlessly and fluidly followed closely behind.

"By the end of it," Tantalus grumbled, "that's exactly what you'll be rolling off the assembly line, Mister Guderian!"

Tantalus pushed his way past the two guards and angrily exited the factory through a side-door. He was barcly a step outside when Junigatsu grabbed hold of his arm. Her firm grip startled him.

"You were warned not to leave the premises," she warned softly.

"I'm not leaving the bloody premises! Get your skinny little hands off me!" He pulled away and pointed to her accusingly.

"I got you to blame for sneaking me out of my homeland and into this God-forsaken piss-hole!"

Tantalus missed the British air, stuffy as it was at times, but he had too much pride in his work, and far too much greed. He had been part of the new weapon concept when he was a junior assistant at an engineering firm closely tied to the Royal Navy, followed through its prolonged gestation period until one of the prototypes was about to be put forth into full production. By then, he had attempted to push his innovations into the design to correct the multitudes of immobilizing mechanical flaws, but was cast aside and demoted from the project for his impertinence by arrogant bean-counters and parliamentarian fat cats.

Shunned from any career prospects, he scraped shillings working in a pistol manufacture just to pay the rent. That all changed when Junigatsu knocked at his door with offerings to his ego that were just too good to be true.

The raunchy motor of an imported Harley-Davidson Model 16F motorcycle cut through the air, just as Guderian stepped out onto the grassy lea between warehouses and airfield. They faced the approaching two-wheeled vehicle as it halted with a skid across the ground; modified with armor plating and saddlebags, it was a rare sight compared to the typical German-made NSU and British Douglas motorcycles often seen zipping about the edges of the battlefield as scouts and couriers.

The biker, Walden Geist, kicked out the stand, shut the engine off, and removed his dusty goggles, revealing fierce azure eyes that pierced through Tantalus. He stood up, towering all those present, and passed a gloved hand across the blondish bristles on his head as he approached. He wore a superb civilian fur-lined coat over a field grey tunic with Saxon cuffs, though most of the Landsturm units still donned the pre-war dark blue uniforms.

Guderian saluted with a click of his heels. [Morning, Generalmajor Geist.]

[Likewise, Oberst Guderian.] Geist eyed Tantalus, as he removed his leather gloves. "Are we out for a little stroll, Mister Tantalus?"

Tantalus had reason to fear everyone in his present company, but the imposing physique and sharp intellect of the Major-General of the 97th Landwehr Regiment made him particularly nervous. Especially when considering that the official records stated there were only ninety-six regiments protecting the homeland. Normally composed of soldiers too old or too young for the warfront, the Landsturm acted as the reservist Home Guard, but this regiment was something else.

"N-No, not at all." Tantalus cleared his throat. "Your workers are making a mockery of your precious super-tank. I'm merely venting."

Geist nodded as a parade of Landsturm assault troopers carrying Gewehr 98 rifles marched behind him, stomping their boots toward the small airfield where a squadron of crimson Fokkers were being prepped from the hangers for flight. The zeppelin assigned to this sector was already patrolling the sky.

"If you wish it, I can have the entire gang summarily executed," Geist suggested with a hint of deadly sarcasm. "Perhaps the lovely Junigatsu here can demonstrate her martial prowess on them, simply for blood sport. Doing so will require me to replenish the workforce, and skilled tradesmen are hard to come by these days due to this blasted 'War to End All Wars'. It will delay this operation by months, time that the Kaiser will not spare, and a mission I will not fail, because of some minor itch from some traitorous Englishman."

Geist's cold tone instilled dread in Tantalus' gut, but the brilliant engineer remained adamant. "You dragged me here to build you a machine that can trample anything being thrown on the battlefield today. I can be bold saying this tank – my brainchild – is ahead of its time! What use is this thing if it breaks down on its own volition, or if it gets knocked out by friendly fire?! If you want this project done right, you give me full control of what happens on that factory floor!"

Geist, switching to his native tongue, turned to Colonel Guderian. [Your thoughts on this matter, Oberst?]

[If we let him near the workers, they will know what we're building here. They will not be allowed to leave...] Guderian considered the possibility carefully. [If it comes to that, one of the troop barracks can be converted as temporary shelter.]

[If they protest, they'll know who to blame.] Geist looked back at Tantalus, ignoring the irritated look on the man's face. "Your request is granted, Mister Tantalus, but I expect results sooner than you anticipate."

"Naturally. The sooner the prototype is rolling, the sooner I can be 'free'." With a scoff, Tantalus returned to the factory, and Junigatsu was only a few steps behind.

The five-hundred-thirty foot zeppelin cast its shadow on the ground as it hovered overhead, the drone of its four Maybach water-cooled piston engines filling the air.

[Despite his ingenuity, he's volatile,] Guderian commented.

Geist removed his coat and draped it over the motorcycle seat. [Keeps him from outliving his usefulness.]

[No one can trust a turncoat. Not the people he betrayed, nor the people who renege his services.]

[He's a soldier of fortune, like the Landsturm, where everything has a price – from loyalty to life." Geist glanced up at the zeppelin, then to Guderian. [The Kaiser needs this tank to conquer the whole of Europe, before the Brits roll out theirs, and we're here to make certain he receives it in full operating capacity. Keep an eye on the Englishman, don't let him falter.]

Guderian nodded, saluted, and briskly followed the others. Geist turned the other way, toward the aircraft hangars.

He laughed quietly to himself at the fortuitus turns of the war. Unlike most high-ranking commanders, he had fought alongside his soldiers at the start of the conflict, during the invasion of Belgium and France, and was injured at the Battle of the Marne when a shrapnel cut across his neck. He witnessed his cousins and closest friends die horribly after an artillery bombardment, and he should have bled out with them, but was saved by random circumstance and divine luck during the German withdrawal. When he recovered back home, he was lauded with medals and promoted, then given the command of a special task force mainly comprised of mercenaries and the army's undesirables with the mandate to suppress anti-war protests, subdue mutineers from the military, and root out communist movements within the industrial complex. At first it seemed like a setback to his reputation for his part in the military defeat, but his successes in the home front earned the trust of the Kaiser above the contentious generals that surrounded him.

He now oversaw clandestine projects with an imperial cash flow, and although the ugly scar across his neck throbbed at the thought that Tantalus' tracked weapon will end the war in Germany's favor, he secretly hoped it will drag on endlessly.

He laughed again to himself. "The war to end all wars..."

Chapter 3

*W*alking side by side with his borrowed horse while holding its reins, Brazen crossed the airfield of the Toul-Croix de Metz Allied aerodrome just as a dozen French Nieuport biplanes lifted off the dusty runway. Still wearing a German uniform, eighty kilometers from Verdun, in the region of Lorraine, and a stone's throw away from the Western Front, he captured the notice of pilots and technicians in the tents and hangars, and it wasn't long before a trio of military policemen pointed their rifles at him.

Brazen complied by slowly lifting his hands. "I'm Sergeant Orin Alastair Brazen of the 32nd Battalion, Canadian Expeditionary Force. I need to speak with the Colonel Ciraud immediately."

One of the pilots from the Canadian division, Walter Cyrus, broke away from his inspection of a Bristol F.2A two-seat reconnaissance fighter with a plain, unassuming livery, and approached without drawing his sidearm.

"It's hard to say you're a friend while wearing the wrong uniform."

Brazen pulled down the backpack from his shoulder and tossed it at the pilot, startling the guards. "My real colors are furled up in there. You can also check my papers while you're at it."

Cyrus dropped the gear with annoyance, and clenched his fists to threaten a swing at Brazen's audacity. "How about a test of wits? Let's see who bleeds first."

The French wing commander, in his iron-pressed horizon blue uniform, quickly intervened between Cyrus and Brazen with two of his armed officers in tow. "Save the bravado for the skies, Lieutenant Cyrus. Check the man's gear for his uniform and documents."

Cyrus scowled at the order, but was submissive. "...Yes, sir."

The wing commander, a rigid, mustachioed disciplinarian, scrutinized Brazen. [What devil brings you from the trenches to drag those muddy boots all over my airfield?] he reprimanded in eloquent Parisienne.

Brazen saluted properly to the superior officer, then replied in the same tongue and inflection. [Colonel Ciraud, sir. You received an urgent dispatch from the War Office not long ago.]

Ciraud became all the more suspicious. [What of it?]

"The Gauntlet has dropped, sir."

The secret phrase, although confusing to everyone who heard it, caught the wing commander by surprise, but only for a moment, before he nodded as if mildly impressed.

"When I got the word down from those pricks at the War Office, I thought they were joking..." Ciraud adjusted the lapel on Brazen's German coat, noting the dried blood in the fabric. "You knew I would've held you under equal suspicion if you had barged in here wearing your real uniform."

Brazen indeed knew, as most nights some soldiers on the frontline lost courage and tried to escape, and if caught, the punishment was to be shot by your own people. "Hard to tell the difference between stragglers and spies."

"Humph." The Colonel let his curiosity about the man and his mission linger, unnerving those under his command. "Very well, get yourself in order, then report to my tent." Ciraud paused a moment, and as an afterthought, he looked over at the MP's. [Lower your rifles, he's one of us.]

Although befuddled, the military policemen lowered their weapons as the Colonel and his officers walked away, and gave Brazen wider berth much to Cyrus' chagrin.

Brazen, glad the confrontation was over, approached Cyrus, and snatched his gear back while handing the pilot the reins to the horse.

"Still learning how to fly, Walter?" Brazen jabbed as he walked past Cyrus.

Cyrus smirked dryly. "At least I got wings, Orin."

With the debrief over, and wearing his CEF drab service tunic with a standing collar and shoulder straps, Brazen stepped out of the wing commander's tent, passing the two guards on station. Nearby, four air mechanics formed an impressive string quartet with two violins, a viola, and a cello. They were performing to the amusement of their fellow comrades and pilots as they gathered around a small bonfire for the evening break.

Fixing his officer's cap, Brazen walked across the airfield to the hangar where Cyrus' reconnaissance fighter was being fueled and loaded by the hangar crew. A large biplane with a span of thirty-nine feet in which its fuselage was nuzzled between the upper and lower wings, and powered by a rushed-out-the-factory Rolls-Royce Falcon engine. Fitted with a synchronized Vickers machine gun on the cockpit, and a defensive Lewis machine gun mounted aft, the fighter was a capable aircraft when all things worked as they should.

Cyrus approached behind him, and angrily turned Brazen around to face him. "I don't know how you convinced Ciraud to assign me to this fool's errand, but he didn't leave me much of a choice."

"You got me wrong," Brazen said, "I didn't recommend you at all."

"Luck of the draw then, huh?" Cyrus wasn't sure whether to feel elated or disappointed.

"Coincidence, I'm sure."

Cyrus scoffed. "This better be worth it."

"According to the records, you're neither a father nor a husband, and there's not much for you to go home to after this war's over." Brazen knew he was being harsh, but he was stating facts. "I won't say it's not a one-way flight, but it doesn't have to be if you keep your head down and don't ask too many questions."

The thought of the long flight over hostile territory brought a tight knot in Cyrus' stomach. "You were on the other side of the trenches already, with German greys and a horse, so why didn't you keep going?"

"I crossed over to get a location," Brazen said, as he put away his cap for a sheepskin-lined, supple leather coat and flying helmet offered to him by one of the air mechanics, "and the mission's time-sensitive. Too far in on foot, and too many Germans in the way."

Cyrus had watched friends die over the last few years, some needlessly, some heroically, and knew the war had changed a lot of good-natured people and turned them into trained murderers. He had known Brazen since their stint in the Legion of Frontiersmen undertaking covert intelligence gathering and counterintelligence operations prior to the breakout of global hostilities, long before the assassination of the Astro-Hungarian heir to the throne that prompted the war that followed, yet the Great War had not changed Brazen a single bit, but only made him better at his job. "If the rumors I hear about you are right, Orin, you can do almost anything. So why bother with me when you can fly her yourself?"

Cyrus pointed to the fighter. "She can reach one hundred-twenty kilometers-an-hour, and climb twenty thousand feet, and her guns are more than a match for those blasted Fokkers. What say you?" He snickered mockingly. "Oh right, you don't care much for planes."

Brazen respected the technology, but at only ten years in the making, he wasn't entirely thrilled with flying on wings made of stitched canvas and lightweight wooden frames.

"Don't bother me, Walter. You can always bow out."

Cyrus was tempted to do just that, but Lady Fortune was never on his side. "The Colonel knew I'm the only pilot on this airfield that can handle a two-seater; the other Bristol boys are either dead or already in the air."

Checking his gear and restocked supplies, Brazen tried not to be distracted by Cyrus' badgering, but understood the animosity stemmed from mission anxiety and buried grudges. "We locked horns in the Legion over matters of opinion, but I got over it."

"Matters of opinion?" Cyrus repeated disdainfully. "You insolent bastard, you screwed up my whole life because you thought what was good for you was good enough for me."

Brazen faced Cyrus, and stared him in the eye. "There's no point for you to be bitter after all these years, Walter, especially when we're fighting on the same side."

"I could've been teaching at Oxford if you hadn't drafted me into this mess."

"You're a pilot now, and you have orders. Will you carry them out, Lieutenant?"

Cyrus bit down his tongue as he stared down Brazen, then wordlessly gave his answer by striding over to his plane and climbing into the cockpit.

Brazen said nothing himself, and followed him aboard.

Chapter 4

Out on the field between the factories and airship hangars, Walden Geist observed the starry night sky through an antique telescope propped on an elevated gun tripod. He was involved in stargazing, not expecting to spot enemy balloons or planes, but sensed Junigatsu's light-footed prowl.

"What a wonder to the eye the stars truly are," he said aloud, preferring to practice his English than butcher his limited grasp of the Japanese language. He pulled away from the telescope, and stood to his full height as he glanced at Junigatsu. "Our esteemed prodigy is sound asleep in his bunk?"

Junigatsu nodded. "He hardly sleeps."

Geist chuckled softly, not entirely earnest with his concerns over Tantalus' mental health. "Guilty minds barely do." He turned his thoughts to more serious matters, one that tied the affairs of two vastly different empires together. "What's your assessment of this operation so far?"

"I agree with Colonel Guderian's theory on the need for such heavy weaponry in an age of unconventional warfare." Junigatsu had no loyalty to the Germans, but like the Landsturm commander, she knew the value of retaining a business relationship. "These 'tanks' will break the deadlock of the trenches in one form another."

"No doubt it will replace the role of cavalry when machine guns have invalidated the dashing Hussar from the field. But, for your people, whom at one point in history prevented the proliferation of guns, choose now to return to arms. Does your emperor retain ambition of his own?"

Junigatsu saw through Geist's twisted charms. "Such knowledge's compartmentalized."

Geist pressed no further. "We'll leave it at that."

The sound of galloping hooves stomping on grass and earth in the eerie night air attracted his attention, and he turned to Zag, an elite Ottoman cavalryman and mounted sniper. Another soldier borrowed from Germany's short list of allies, the bearded Turk was lighter in complexion than most of his countrymen, of average height and build with dark hair and eyes. He wore a khaki infantry uniform with a bandolier, boots, and spurs, and distinctive kabalak – a helmet with bound cloth which could be let down and fastened around the chin.

[What brings you at this hour, Ottoman Zag?] Geist queried in German.

Zag expertly brought his elegant brown horse to a halt before Geist, and dipped his chin in salute before producing a sealed letter. [A message from one of your operatives in the frontline,] he responded in native Turkic.

Geist took the letter and opened it, gladdened that his knowledge of the Turk's language was more practical than his Japanese. His lips formed a faint grin as he read the content hastily handwritten on the sheet of paper.

[It's a warning...] he said, confirming the information's validity through particular purposeful mutations in the vowels and hashmarks along the edges of the letter. [British Intelligence has finally caught up.]

Zag welcomed the challenge, as it was better than hunting wild game in the German countryside. He was too overqualified for this posting as liaison, and Geist knew it well.

[Step up security around the perimeter,] Geist ordered in Turkic.

Zag complied with the command, spurred his horse about, and raced off.

With Junigatsu waiting to be brought up to speed on the new developments, Geist continued reading the letter aloud. "The first tank has been deployed at Flers-Courcellete, and for the first time in wretched human warfare, it engaged in battle... with limited success."

"The French and British are getting desperate," Junigatsu noted.

Geist agreed. "The lines are drawn, it's no longer a race for the coveted apple of historians for being first." He folded the letter, turned away from his telescope and walked toward the main armament factory. Junigatsu followed in step.

"Wake poor Tantalus and his work crew," Geist said with renewed conviction. "This project will continue around the clock by threat of force or otherwise."

Chapter 5

*B*razen recalled a day in 1895 when he was ten years old, growing up on a samurai estate in Osaka Prefecture, not far from the port-city of Osaka itself. Completing his kenjutsu and iaido exercises for that morning, learning the importance of footwork, and responding quickly to sudden attacks, he joined his adoptive grandmother, Lady Minori, in the drawing room, and knelt respectfully before her. A prominent woman in her forties, hailing from a sustained lineage of successful merchantmen, she had married into a family with a long-standing samurai tradition. After her husband's passing several years before, she carried on both legacies, and tendered the lessons on to her daughters, and to her adopted son.

Wearing a traditional kimono, Minori smiled warmly as she addressed young Brazen, prompting him to sit up. They sat in a room tiled with tatami mats, and shoji-style latticework wooden walls inset with tough, translucent paper adorned with masterful artwork depicting natural landscapes and ancient battles. There was little furniture, except for a funerary tablet inscribed with Tamashii's name, Minori's husband, and a splendid tiger tail tachi koshirae, a two-hundred year-old slung sword designed for mounted combat, placed vertically on a wooden rack with its brass pommel, or kabuto-gane, resting at the bottom. The rack was heavily lacquered and decorated *with gold flecked heraldic crests and a detailed charging samurai on horseback.*

Another sword, a katana in its simple wooden scabbard was placed beside Lady Minori. She regarded the boy as a wealth of joy in her life, but as social customs and rigid upbringing go, she held back expressing such sentiments outright. Her eyes spoke volume while she remained dignified with bent knees and a straight back.

[Little One, it's been three days since we buried your good mother,] she said softly. [It is not an easy thing to live with, but you may lean on my strength when you need to. I will keep my promise to her and to you, to raise you as my own.]

The language was still novel and complex to him, but after three years of immersion, he was able to express himself. [You are my grandmother. I am grateful... I will always be grateful.]

Minori smiled warmly, gingerly picking up the katana, and handing it in proper tradition to the child, with her left hand holding the far end of the wrapped hilt – the tsuka – firmly with the sword's enclosed edge facing herself. [This is Sigh. It belonged to one whom I once loved, and now I give it to one whom I love equally.]

Young Brazen took the katana with mixed awe and uncertainty. His eyes were drawn to the sword, daring to pull the hilt from the scabbard, and revealing its sharp, broken blade.

Overcome with sadness, he sheathed the blade, respectfully set it down, and surprised Lady Minori as he broke etiquette and hugged her. His tears were bound to both love and grief.

Minori wrapped her arms around him, and held him close and tightly so he could hear her beating heart....

The turbulence drafting on the reconnaissance fighter's wings interrupted Brazen's soothing reminiscence, as well as his rendering of a quintessential katana's anatomical breakdown with connotations in Japanese calligraphy. He glanced up at the cockpit ahead as Cyrus piloted the plane through wisps of low-lying clouds.

Wearing his anti-splinter goggles, Cyrus looked over his shoulder with a sly grin as Brazen put away his journal. "Hard to draw straight lines at this height."

Brazen offered no retort, and peered over to the distant ground below. There was still a lot of small towns, plains, and forests unscathed by the war, but a whole lot more that was churned and scarred by bombs and flames.

"Are we flying past German borders?"

"Only the borders they've annexed from the war." Cyrus occasionally glanced up at the sun and higher clouds in case a German ace decided to dive at them. "We're still half a day away from the lion's den." He looked down at the instrument panel, and tapped the gauges. "We might need to make a stopover to refuel."

Although Cyrus was serious on matters on mechanical maintenance, he had the habit of pushing his limits, and crashing from this height was not the lackluster demise Brazen envisioned for himself. "I'm almost disappointed we haven't run into enemy planes yet."

Cyrus enjoyed throwing the occasional verbal jab at Brazen, but sometimes it was given in return. "Don't give up your hopes now," he said sourly. "What were you writing?"

Brazen studied the horizon around them. "What better way to preserve the past than to put it down in ink."

"A memoir by an above-average infantryman – sounds fancy. Where do you get your inspiration?" Although Cyrus' sarcasm was misplaced, he was also curious. "I remember back then, when you were a little more human, you told me your father passed away when you were eight years-old?"

"He worked as a captain's first mate ferrying lumber and other supplies in and out of the Great Lakes when a storm capsized his boat." Brazen paused, exhaling that dreadful moment from his youth. "His creditors chased my Mom and me out of our home until an opportunity came by across the Pacific. We lived in Japan for a time..." Something in the distance ahead of them caught his eye, but still too far to identify. "You never said what happened to the observer that sat second fiddle to you. Was he promoted?"

Cyrus grimaced at the question, also spotting the aberration at his 11 o'clock. "It was our second flight out; got jumped by a trio of Albatros Threes' with some colorful paint schemes. Shot one down, and had to evade the other two. The poor sergeant that sat in your seat had his restraints crap out when I turned the plane in a corkscrew, and the man fell out head-first." He adjusted his fighter's velocity and angle. "His body's rotting away somewhere between France and Belgium."

Brazen re-checked his harness after hearing that dreadful story, noting now a dark blot hovering at a lower altitude. "Is that what I think it is?"

Cyrus smiled devilishly, as if some voluptuous bar maiden presented him a hot meal and a pint of draft beer. "A German balloon, from the looks of it. Probably carrying bombs or listening devices."

Cyrus eased the F.2A down for closer inspection, and the dark blot became a blimp-shaped air platform. The two German balloon operators took notice of their fast approach with mixed confusion and panic. Down below, the crews manning the anti-aircraft guns scrambled.

Brazen secured the flat pan magazine on the Lewis machine gun, and made certain it was properly chambered. "It got lots of guns protecting it."

"Target of opportunity."

Cocking back the lever handle to the Vickers machine gun, and manually loading the first cartridge from the belt into the firing system, Cyrus drove his plane directly behind the balloon and delivered a barrage that punctured the non-rigid airframe from astern across the entire length of its portside. He pulled away in time as the modified Ehrhardt field guns pounded the skies in an attempt to scare him away.

Although the flak was out of range, the airbursts from each exploding shell shook the plane. Brazen was not amused by Cyrus' daredevil flying.

"Get us back on course! You're spending fuel we don't have!"

"It's the price for renown!" With a fiery spirit, Cyrus pivoted the reconnaissance fighter around for another pass, skewing in an unpredictable pattern to avoid being traced by the gunners below. He lowered altitude to strafe the ventral side of the balloon, skidding past the stabilizer fin to the small open-sided gondola where the two operators desperately defended their position with a pair of pistols.

The F.2A's bullets, spat from the Vickers machine gun, mercilessly tore across the balloon's underside, and severed some of the tethers that not only anchored the balloon down ground-side, but tied the gondola to the airframe. The two operators were catapulted from the balloon, and tumbled to their deaths several hundred feet below.

Passing the balloon, Cyrus committed a barrel-roll and swung around for a final assault. This time, he held down the trigger on the Vickers, and raked the faltering balloon's topside until something inside ignited and an explosion ensued.

The balloon deflated as flames gradually consumed its outer layers, and dropped from the sky in pieces onto the anti-aircraft guns.

Cyrus hollered victoriously, insensitive to the heinous deaths of the balloon crew and the gunners that failed to stop him. "One more for the record!"

"Get us going before the Fokkers get here," Brazen advised, almost glad the mechanical rumbling of the fighter's engine deafened him to the screams of the men burning alive below.

"You're not easily impressed," Cyrus chided, still elated at his small triumph, and making a mental note on the time and location to officially secure the score.

"No, I'm not. Get us out of here before we drop out of the sky after those poor suckers."

Cyrus scoffed at Brazen's heartless remark, but didn't let it spoil his excitement. He circled high over his smoldering kill twice before resuming course into enemy territory.

Chapter 6

Slowly taking shape, the massive tank slumbered in the deep shadows of the armament factory, sunlight from a skylight overhead illuminating the heavy rusted chains that leashed the monstrosity in place. Progress was stalled by angry welders and steel workers, all of them shouting and cursing at Tantalus. Although their wails were in German, the British engineer knew when he was being threatened.

He cowered behind an experimental version of the schwere Maschinengewehr 08 machine gun on a Scarff ring mount normally used on fighter planes, becoming angrier and impatient at the loss of precious time and effort.

"We need to get this machine off the assembly line, you whelps!" Tantalus tried to put demanding power behind his words, but was underwhelming at best. "Get back to work!"

He glanced up at Guderian on the central catwalk, who was enjoying the spectacle at a safe distance from the mob with a few frowning provost guards at his side.

"Do something, you stuck-up bastard!" Tantalus yelled, shaking his fist at Guderian, as he was about to be surrounded by the workers.

Goaded by his crew, the veteran assembler and foreman with a scarred burn mark above his right ear, threw a short steel rod at Tantalus, which missed cleanly as Junigatsu pulled Tantalus aside. The rod hit the far wall and clattered to the floor with a loud, leaden clang.

One of the large warehouse doors was pushed open, and a contingent of Landsturm infantrymen with rifles slung over their shoulders marched between the workmen and Tantalus, stopping their advance but not their protests.

Geist approached Guderian on the catwalk, casually glancing down at the ruckus. [Are you letting the mob dictate the rules, Oberst Guderian?]

Guderian straightened his back before the ranking officer. [I was simply observing, Generalmajor, and deciding how best to defuse the situation.]

[Walk me through your logic,] Geist demanded, appeasing the Colonel's tactical mindset.

[As you predicted, the workers are protesting their forced confinement to this facility. Now that you've put Tantalus on the floor with them, compounded with the rigors of round-the-clock shifts, they snapped.]

Geist looked to the workmen, and the majority of the rabble now directed their frustrations at him. [I keep forgetting why they've put you here, that is until I realize you're the one drawing up the reports to the Kaiser on developing new tactics with the use of these tanks. Otherwise, you're as useless as the bureaucrats.]

Not caring for being called a politician, Guderian cleared his throat, and did his best to retain his confident poise. [All in all, Generalmajor, tackle the source and the rest will follow. The foreman's in charge of relaying orders to his crew, and inexorably, he's the one leading this mob.] He rubbed an itch on his chin. [I was debating whether or not to take the zeppelin and the Baron's Fokker squadron to raze the nearby town where some of these workers hail from. Our pilots and gunners are getting complacent so far behind the battle lines, and could use the exercise.]

Geist agreed on that last notion. [I may yet give you leeway on that regard, Oberst.] Clasping his hands at the small of his back, he descended the wrought iron steps to the floor – each methodical footfall sounding loudly over the cacophony.

The workmen gradually quieted down as Geist approached them, and Tantalus summed up the courage to break away from Junigatsu's protection.

"This is not something you can blame me for! You drove them mad, now I expect you to put them back in line!"

"Quiet."

Such a simple word, yet how Geist said it was enough for Tantalus to humbly bite down his tongue.

[We don't mind the work, Generalmajor Geist,] the foreman said, [but you can't deliberately keep us from our families! We demand to be allowed to leave the premises!]

Geist turned his eyes to the foreman. [Demand? I thought you were made aware why you workers are here to begin with.] He held out a hand to the shadowy mechanical beast behind them. [Are you not loyal sons and brothers? Doesn't the safeguard of your empire interest you?]

The foreman stood his ground. [There's no loyalty without the pay, and most of us are too old for the front. We are workers, not indentured servants—] He pointed accusingly at Tantalus. [Especially not under this English traitor's leash!]

[You were kept from the trenches because of your skills, and since you are just simple-minded workers, then I expected nothing less and nothing more of you. You disappoint.] He turned to Tantalus, switching language. "What was scheduled for this shift, Mister Tantalus?"

Tantalus was at first confused, but glanced at the machine gun. "Uh, we needed to test these guns before we mounted them on the chassis."

"Then do so." Geist tuned to the infantrymen, switching back to German. [Hold the foreman against the wall.]

Two of the infantrymen quickly seized hold of the foreman, while the rest raised their weapons to keep the startled work crew from lashing out. Passing the robust sMG 08, the soldiers threw the foreman against the wall of the factory where the steel rod had struck, and backed away with their rifles aimed.

"You may test the gun, Tantalus," Geist ordered.

Tantalus was often accused of being mad with his projects, a baseless proponent of the war industry, but never crossed that bloody line. "What are you doing?"

"Re-establishing control. Fire, now."

Tantalus hesitated, and Geist pushed him aside to pull the trigger himself. The machine gun, infamous for its atrocious toll on the Allied forces at the start of the war, unleashed its firepower, repeatedly striking the foreman and puncturing holes in the factory wall with fervent abandon. After countless spent bullet shells cluttered the floor, Geist released the trigger.

The barrel smoked as the gun's belt feed creaked to a halt.

[The body will remain there until you resume work,] Geist said to the workers, and pointed at one amongst them. [You're the foreman now.]

Geist calmly left with his armed company, and in moments, the workers grumbly scattered back to their jobs.

Chapter 7

*T*he reconnaissance fighter was parked within a narrow clearing in Lower Mundat, a dense and diverse forest of spruce, pine, beech, and oak between the pre-war borders of France and Germany. Holding up a small lantern, Cyrus inspected the plane for damages, running his hand along its painted surface with certain care. There were small perforations, but nothing that would hinder the plane's aerodynamics, and easily patched with the sewing kit he had stashed away along with the extra fuel and food rations.

The F.2A was a large aircraft with a sizeable wingspan, and the Rolls-Royce Falcon engine that kept it airborne was powerful, but suffered some mechanical setbacks that had been fixed with gum, spit, and tape by the capable air mechanics back at the Toul-Croix de Metz aerodrome. Most of the surviving F.2A fighters had their powerplant replaced by the more able Sunbeam Arab, but Cyrus had opted to keep his plane as it was, even its nondescript livery, about as original as when it left the factory. Even when the grumblings of a whole new iteration of the Bristol scout fighter with added protection for the lower wing and improved engine rolled out in practical form to replace the older variations, he would fight tooth and nail to keep this F.2A.

He passed a hand on the row of painted kill scores just below the cockpit entryway, eight planes in all, and reminded himself to add a balloon for the count once he was finished with the repairs. Unlike other pilots, both friend and foe, he chose not to adorn his plane with an insignia, like a hat in the ring, a poker hand, or pin-up bombshell. He kept his vanity in more subtle ways, daring rival pilots to get close enough to see the hashmarks chalked on the side of his fighter's cockpit. Though he craved the thrill of the kill, it was something he would never openly admit.

Brazen approached, his Lee-Enfield rifle at the ready, and was keenly observing his surroundings for enemy scouts. "The perimeter's clear for the time being. We can't risk a fire, so tonight, we're eating a cold meal."

"Nothing like chilly beans." Cyrus was already missing the comforts offered at the airbase, courtesy of the French commanders who knew pilots had a lower survival rate than the army regulars, and were harder to replace.

"Better turn out the light," Brazen cautioned, "and use your night eyes."

"I'm almost done." Cyrus ducked under the starboard wing, satisfied with his inspection. "Bird looks fine, but she needs every last drop of fuel we got left in the canister."

"That means there's no return trip."

Cyrus accepted the implication with some dread, though his flight partner had no particular concern. "You almost sound relieved."

"I don't mind planes," Brazen admitted, "so long as they fly a straight line."

"If you manage to pull this one off," Cyrus said with a stifled laugh, "then you can hitch a ride on some truck back to friendly territory." He lovingly patted the fighter, having lost count of the hours spent flying in it. "I plan to stick around with this fellow until one of us gives out."

"I'll keep your suggestion in mind, Walter... and maybe you should too if you're still planning to become an oil baron after the war." Brazen strolled past Cyrus, snatching up the emptied canteens from their supplies, and headed toward the trees.

"Watch out for the wolves, good Orin," Cyrus harangued. "The scraggy ones on this side of the crossing are a nasty bunch."

"Don't wait up for me," Brazen said. "And shut off that light."

Evening had passed into a moonless night, with starlight streaming through the leafy canopy, and Brazen felt his way through the winding paths between ancient spruce trees. His steps were deliberately slow and steady as he trailed a predator in the woods not far from his position. Barely a sound was made as his boots crushed the grass and old roots beneath the soles of his boots.

Ahead of him was a lone timber wolf, an omega shunned from his pack, quietly drinking from a shallow creek that snaked through the forest. Its beautiful silver fur bristled from the scattered light reflecting off the surface of the stream.

Brazen prowled behind the animal, the breeze against him and hiding his scent. He carefully removed his prize Mauser pistol from its holster, and aimed its long, lean barrel until its cold, black muzzle was nearly an inch away from the wolf's furry right ear.

Still, the wolf was unaware of Brazen's proximity, until he pulled the trigger. Without bullets in the chamber, the pistol's solid hammer strike startled the animal from its peaceful indulgence. It coiled back fearfully, and snarled in annoyance, but rather than attack, it scampered off into the wilderness.

Engaging the safety switch with his thumb, Brazen locked the 8-round box magazine back into the Mauser, and slipped the pistol back in its holster. Grabbing the canteen from his gear, he filled it up in the creek....

Chapter 8

Sitting atop his plane's upper wing with one leg up and tucked in, Cyrus broodingly contemplated old thoughts with thousands of stars over his head, and a loaded Colt Government .45 with an elusive blue sheen in hand. He had won the gun off a gamble with another Canadian pilot, after he had downed more aircraft than the other officer after seven sorties. Sadly, on the seventh flyby, the other pilot crashed on the runway, but kept his end of the bargain before dying of his burns. It was hard to forget things like that, and a little bit of dark humor between pilots and soldiers helped desensitize the violent death around them, though he couldn't remember the joke on this particular occasion.

Deep in his rumination, he vaguely noticed Brazen exit the woods.

Brazen, dropping the canteen beside the rest of his gear, looked up at Cyrus. Attrition without respite too often pushed men to the brink of despair, no matter how valiant their repertoire. "Don't think about it."

Cyrus glanced down at Brazen, his voice coarse. "Think about what?"

"I know why you flyboys keep track of your kills, but keeping record just makes it all come back around."

"I don't have anything worth a legend, Orin, just eight planes and yesterday's balloon..." Cyrus sighed, borne out of mental exhaustion. His comradery with Brazen was a cautious one at best, yet the man saw through his ghost with all its flaws. He had added his kill count on the side of the cockpit using some chalk, and he could scarcely imagine the butcher's bill on Brazen's canvas. "Do you... get a joy out of it?"

"Joy? No. It's war; it's us or them." Brazen crossed his arms from the chillness of the night, and leaned against the fighter's tail. "Maybe one day our sins are wreathed in poppies and forgiven by the poets."

After a moment of contemplation, Cyrus wondered. "Why didn't you stay in Japan?"

"I would've..." Brazen said, remembering the kind encouragement of his adopted grandmother and her daughters. "I was only fifteen, and wanted to find my own way, but the Imperial government was becoming increasingly xenophobic as it continued to modernize its infrastructure, as well as its military. So I returned to my father's homeland—"

"And joined the Legion; that's where and when we met," Cyrus interjected. "Two young idiots without a plan."

Brazen wanted to laugh, but took the effort to hold it back. "*I* had a plan, at least."

"No, you didn't. We both impressed enough people with our stupidity that we landed a couple of free tickets to London; you became a special constable, and I went off to university."

Brazen didn't argue the point, as his commendations in London eventually attracted the notice of the Secret Service

Bureau, and had since bounced from one assignment to another since 1912. So many hair-raising stories he wished he could share with Cyrus, but he was unable to under an oath he took quite seriously.

"...To think that my foster parents were happy to see me off," Cyrus reminisced bitterly, "knowing I won't be any more of a burden to them." He cursed under his breath, as the bitterness snowballed outward. "And you had me go broke before I was able to pay off my scholarship, doctorate and all, forcing me to run from my guarantors by signing up to this shit."

"I don't know why you're still blaming me, when it's obvious you're the one who risked all your savings for... what? Some black gold you thought you found in the Maracaibo Basin?" Brazen minced no words for Cyrus' own benefit. Better an angry pilot than a miserable one. "Back when you valued my friendship, you came to me for advice, and as a friend I gave you exactly what you needed to hear. Nothing was going to budge you against a decision you already made. You just needed someone to ease your conscience."

"Could've been rich in the Americas... Damn those debtors..." There was another pause, as Cyrus gritted his teeth together. "Taking risks, it's the only way I know I'm still alive. This..." He gestured to the star-filled night, gun still in hand. "This isn't what I wanted for myself, I want to go home, earn an honest living, settle down and plant roots, and I'm damned because I know there's no way I'll get any restitution for all these years I've wasted."

"You think I want this?" Brazen resolutely buried his feelings, keeping the mission at hand, and that meant Cyrus back in the cockpit seat. "You got wings, and you're not afraid to use them. I saw the look in your eye when you were flying circles around your kill, and you loved the feeling. And you hate yourself for it."

Cyrus grimaced at the truth of it. "Live with it, right?"

Brazen nodded assuredly, then took one of the filled canteens from his gear and tossed it to Cyrus. "Better to die with some self-respect than none."

Brazen grabbed his bed roll and blanket, hoping to rest a bit before the dawn break, and Cyrus took his words to heart. Putting the Colt away, he popped open the canteen and drank up.

Chapter 9

A rudimentary bunk had been set up for Tantalus amidst crates and barrels in one of the storage rooms inside the armament factory, but he rarely slept peacefully. Tossing and turning, the sheets wrapped themselves around his legs; the pillow was on the floor, alongside the clutter of schematics and scribbled papers.

His eyelids were tightly shut, and his brow furrowed with frustration. He dreamt of pistons, steam, and gears. The scalding heatwave and choking fumes of the beastly engine churning within the claustrophobic confines of an armored shell, robbing him of breath, stinging his eyes, frying his skin against the cherry-hot rivets.

In a feverish trance, the sponsons turned on him, the glaring abyss of the rifled muzzles staring down at him like a hundred eyes. Unseen forces loaded the guns, and were about to fire all at once.

"No... Don't... Don't... NO!" Tantalus woke up in a startle. "Don't shoot!"

Sitting up and panting with cold sweat and shallow breaths, Tantalus, already terrified and muddled from the nightmare, jumped up in fright as Junigatsu appeared out of the shadows ready to strike at the supposed intruder.

Tantalus grasped his chest, trying to calm his stammering heart, and scowled at the Japanese woman. "There's no one here for you to protect me from!"

Junigatsu checked the storage room, her guard still up, and was naturally suspicious. "I heard you screaming."

"I wasn't screaming!" Tantalus yelled out of embarrassment, tossing the covers off his legs. He had a scornful, judgmental mother – God rest her soul – and he had no need for another. "I was just... having a nightmare, that's all."

He threw his legs over the edge of the bed, sat up hunched, and rummaged through his unkempt hair nervously. Junigatsu eased her stance, putting away the tanto as she gave the storage room another cursory glance.

"This isn't the first night you suffer sleeplessness," Junigatsu psychoanalyzed, resorting to a discomforting part of her special training to ensure her mission stayed on track. "You've been carrying a heavy burden since we crossed the English Channel."

Tantalus laughed, rather miserably. He knew there was no one on this Earth who cared about his well-being other than himself, but she made a convincing effort. "Please, I got no remorse for what I've done. I know I'm a dead man, it's a question of who gets to me first... No, what occupies my mind is something else, something that divides the likes of me from the likes of you." Giving himself to his base urges, he eyed his guardian's feminine figure with sinister intent. "I dream of numbers, of equations that permeate the future landscape."

Junigatsu approached his bed, noticing the gleam of something metallic on the mattress.

"This tank will be my greatest achievement, and it will surpass anything those bastards back at home draw up," Tantalus divulged freely, ensnared by the magnum opus burning a hole in his mind, and stirring his loins.

Acting on lust, with this strange woman so close to him, he ran his hand on the back of Junigatsu's muscular leg. "And they will regret turning my genius away when the treads of my machine trample over the wrecks of theirs."

Junigatsu viciously jabbed her palm against his chin, knocking him flat on his back and bouncing against the bunk. "Fleeting thoughts of iron do nothing to deter the nature of men."

She appropriated the hidden Browning 1900 pistol from the mattress, and dismantled it as Tantalus cursed in anger at his hurt jaw and pride. When she moved away, he struggled back on his elbows with a devilish laugh.

"Do you know of an old Norse myth," Tantalus spat out with a bit of blood trickling from a split lower lip, "where Odin decides to keep the great wolf, Fenrir, chained in his hall, knowing it will be the instrument of his demise?"

He continued laughing to himself, as if falling to madness, and Junigatsu let him be, securing the lock on the door to his room.

Walking down the corridor to the foreman's office, the echo of the madman's laughter fading away within the walls and piping, she stepped inside to find Guderian studying another set of blueprints unfolded on the desk under the light of a banker's lamp. Shadows played on Guderian's face, making him appear far more sinister than his usual deportment.

"Calmed him have you?" Guderian inquired, his eyes turning up at her as she approached.

Junigatsu loudly dropped the dissembled gun parts she appropriated from Tantalus onto the desk, and on top of the tank blueprints which she suspected was the copy of the original that was stolen from the British naval shipyards where the prototype was constructed.

"This is the second time I've caught him with a hidden weapon," Junigatsu stated firmly. "He's unhinged; we can't risk him turning a gun on himself or us."

Guderian was not at all interested in Tantalus' state of mind, or Junigatsu's concerns. His eyes returned to the designs, imagining a blitzkrieg across the European mainland with these machines. "The brilliant idiot has death as his companion; possession of a little gun might ease his glaring insecurities."

The Colonel was about to push away the gun parts that blocked his view of the schematics, when Junigatsu slammed her palm down to keep them planted.

She looked straight in his eye now that she had his attention. "Tell your guards to stop taking bribes from the engineer to smuggle him weapons, or the Major-General will take a closer inspection of the armory, and realize his weak-willed officers are profiteering off the missing ordnance."

Guderian replied to her threat with a lopsided grin. "The women of our Deutschland are strong, and more than willing to fight with the men, but instead are delegated to the hospitals and factories. I've been to your empire years ago, to help train artillery units, and I was amazed at how your elegant culture valued method and harmony, yet treated their scrawny, little women as second-class denizens. Seeing you now, Lady Junigatsu, standing toe-to-toe with heartless men twice your size, then you must be quite special to have been honored with this task by your Emperor."

"Watch what line you step on, Colonel."

"Always," he replied. "I will reprimand the guards, as requested, but most of these men are bored so far from the frontline, enough to gamble and pilfer under our commander's nose, and so I make no guarantees."

Chapter 10

With the dawn on them, Cyrus hastened to pour the last of the fuel into the reconnaissance fighter's reserve, while Brazen stowed their gear aboard.

"This should be enough to get us to our destination and a bit more," Cyrus said, keeping an eye on the teetering needle in the fuel gauge. "Considering you know exactly where we're heading."

Brazen tied down the last of the backpacks behind the observer's seat. "If the aerial surveys are still up to date, there are a few structures a hundred clicks east from here that might be what I'm looking for."

"No chance you can be more specific?"

"We're looking for factories, and the only details I can give you is that there's a turncoat involved."

"Sounds bad enough already." On the last drop, Cyrus tossed the emptied canister deep in the cover of a nearby brush with the hopes of maximizing the fighter's range with less weight, even if it wasn't much.

The thrumming of aircraft engines whizzing by somewhere in the distance against the quietness of the early morning caught their attention.

"That sounds bad too," Brazen remarked, searching the sky, though the planes were still out of sight.

"Patrols," Cyrus said, recognizing the aural cues of enemy aircraft well enough to warrant some haste. "We better get off the ground."

Cyrus climbed into the cockpit and ran checks on the instrument panel, then tested the controls on the rudder, ailerons, and elevators. Brazen moved to the front of the craft and readied to spin the propeller.

Prepping the ignition, Cyrus looked to Brazen past the target reticle on the Vickers gun and the engine cowling. "Contact!"

Brazen gave the two-blade wooden propeller a hard shove, and the ignition cranked, spinning the blade, and waking the engine. He kicked off the rocks under the tires of the landing gear, then climbed into the observer's seat behind the pilot. In no time, the F.2A was roving across the clearing until momentum lifted it off the ground and into clear skies.

Geist drove his motorcycle across the flock of berthed Fokker Eindecker III monoplanes parked along the side of the airfield not far from the factories, instilling brief salutes from the mechanics and German-Austrian pilots that manned them. Beyond the planes, the gargantuan, ochre-skinned zeppelin crept out from its equally enormous hangar in preparation for its routine flight; the staccato sound of its powerful engines filled the air.

Hearing melancholy Austrian verismo opera over the mechanical drone of his motorcycle engine, he brought the bike to a sharp halt before Baron Justus – a lauded Austrian officer risen from the obscure middle class – kicked the stand and shut the engine. He dismounted and approached the ace pilot, who sat comfortably on his plush chair under the shade of his fighter's wing, while drinking a pint of local brew and listening to music on a gramophone, whose revolving record pushed sound through a large, flaring brass horn.

Geist glanced to the Baron's unusual Fokker monoplane; heavily armed with three synchronized guns, and painted bone-white with a grey lozenge pattern and German Cross.

The sharp-eyed veteran smiled in greeting, raising his glass to Geist. [Good morning, sir. Some blonde beer from the town over?]

[I don't drink, Freiherr Justus,] Geist replied. [Alcohol is an indulgence, and ultimately a distraction.] He examined the painted canvas of the Baron's unique Fokker fighter. [Your craft's a rare sight. White is the true color of death.]

Justus gave a toast to his plane with great pride. [An experiment in subtlety is all it is, Generalmajor. Whatever I can do to make it harder for unfriendly eyes to see me.]

Geist nodded in understanding. Too often he had seen impressive liveries of reds, blues, and yellows on fighter planes, but chivalrous plumes usually came at a price of being easily spotted by rival pilots and jittery gunners.

[An enemy scout plane was spotted heading across our borders, riding hard on the west wind. It shot down one our observation balloons, and damaged some artillery in the process.]

Baron Justus quietly saluted the boldness of the enemy pilot before taking another sip of beer. [Loss of life is no issue.]

Geist didn't care for the Baron's tone, even if tools of war were more replaceable than trained soldiers, though no less costly. [Do you keep your wits sharp with your tongue, Freiherr?]

[Apologies...] Justus stood up at attention before his commander. [A scout, you say? French? Commonwealth?]

[Doesn't make a difference. I want it destroyed before it even sets sight on this place.]

Although Justus knew it did quite make a difference of knowing who the enemy was and what he flew, drawing upon the limitations of a man's prowess and courage, and the mechanical pros and cons of the machine, he did not want to argue the point with Geist. [Ah, then you believe it's the British operative we were warned about.]

Geist was normally patient, but it ran thin at times with officers who knew more than they let on, yet insisted on dragging out the point. [I want that plane in flames, Freiherr. The sooner, the better.]

[It will be done.] The Baron finished the rest of his glass, set it aside the gramophone, and stopped the music. Tightening his white pilot scarf, and his tanned leather gloves, he saluted Geist, then turned to the pilots standing by their planes. [Gentlemen, we have an appointment with the skies! An angel has gone rogue, and we're here to clip its wings!]

[In God's name! Long live the Kaiser!] the pilots answered in unison.

The Baron smirked knowingly at Geist as the pilots scrambled to the planes. He walked regally to his white Fokker as the mechanics prepared it for the runway – his lined, leather coat flapping with determination in his wake....

Chapter 11

*W*ith the forest far beneath them, the Bristol F.2A reconnaissance fighter cut through the clouds with barbarous expediency. While Cyrus concentrated on navigating the air currents, Brazen probed the skies for enemy craft. Ahead of them, storm clouds were brewing for an early afternoon downpour.

The sound of propellers reached them before the Fokker squadron appeared like crimson blots against the blue.

"Ten o'clock!" Brazen pointed out over the wind and engine chatter, and readied the Lewis machine gun. "Can we outrun them?!"

Cyrus banked the fighter to face the squadron head-on. His eyes began to notice the shape and colors of the leading aircraft, which a moment ago had been virtually invisible. "Until we run out of fuel..." he said, finally recognizing the markings on the lead craft. "The white Fokker, it's Baron Justus' squadron."

News, both tragic and heroic, travelled sporadically in the trenches, and Brazen had heard of plenty of ace pilots by name and reputation in passing, but within the pilot aristocracy on both sides of the conflict, names and reputations were far more significant. "Is he any good?"

"Good enough," Cyrus replied ruefully. The 'ace' system was never officially embraced by any warring military organization, though five or more confirmed kills was the gentlemen's agreement between pilots to earn the honorarium. Accolades differed between nations, and even within squadrons, and that either meant a collection silver trophies with the names of the fallen, a parade in town ending with a drunken night with the ladies, or informally given a new title worthy of recognition by both friend and foe.

"Very few pilots are given the privilege of being called a baron," Cyrus supplemented. "Here they come."

The eleven pilots tagging Baron Justus' white Fokker opened fire on the lone reconnaissance fighter, and in turn Cyrus skewed his flight pattern to avoid a direct hit, then barreled through them – forcing the monoplanes to break formation.

The F.2A came about sharply and trailed one of the rear-formation Fokkers with a plain olive paint scheme, unloading a barrage from the Vickers machine gun that shredded the enemy fuselage apart. The Fokker pilot attempted to deviate out of harm's way, but Cyrus stayed sharp on him until his pounding cleaved the rudder from its tail hinges.

Losing stability and catching fire, the damaged Fokker descended uncontrollably to the ground.

Two crimson Fokkers converged behind the F.2A, angered by the loss of their comrade, and shelled the air with bullets. Despite Cyrus' skillful maneuvering, the starboard wing was pierced repeatedly. Brazen fired back with the Lewis gun in short bursts, keeping the enemy pilots from gaining a clear run on them.

Jamming hard on the rudders, Cyrus doubled-back and barrel-rolled, turning upside-down to use the Vickers machine gun on the left-most crimson Fokker – strafing the enemy plane from spinner to rudder and killing the pilot instantly.

Brazen, hanging on to his seat by force, and unable to use the Lewis effectively, shot the second pilot in the neck with his Mauser pistol.

With two more Fokkers tumbling down, Cyrus reverted the F.2A back on its proper orientation with the horizon, and arced widely to starboard across the reformed enemy squadron under the Baron's lead.

Baron Justus motioned one of his senior wingmen to detach from formation and attack. The pilot concurred without question, speeding after the reconnaissance fighter, and firing away. With the offered distraction, Justus gave another silent command to the rest of his squadron, and they all dispersed in separate directions like a blossoming flower.

With the enemy encroaching in all directions, Brazen replaced the Mauser with a fragmentation hand grenade that was also known as a Mill's bomb. He ducked as bullets pierced the dorsal frame from behind, and sparked against the Lewis machine gun.

"Watch your six!" Brazen warned.

Cyrus banked left, and the trailing Fokker pilots answered by banking right. Their widely spaced pivoting brought them about in an encirclement until both planes levelled their wings and faced each other.

Picking up speed, neither pilot gave in to cowardice, and fired away with their guns. Brazen, measuring the narrowing distance between the planes, pulled the pin from the grenade and silently counted to four. Bullets whizzed past, and when it seemed both planes were going to ram into each other, Cyrus wheeled to starboard.

With expert marksmanship, Brazen tossed the live grenade into the Fokker's cockpit just as the planes flew past each other barely a few feet apart. The startled enemy pilot had only a heartbeat to react before the explosion split the fuselage apart. The tail, wings, and engine scattered away in all directions.

The victory was cut short as Baron Justus' white Fokker screamed down on the F.2A from above, its guns ripping the port aileron clean off the wing.

Cyrus worked the controls to ease the sudden strain on the joystick and pedals, but had little room to maneuver as the rest of the Fokker squadron surrounded them from all sides. Their guns, wary of accidentally hitting their fellow monoplanes, scraped the F.2A with each pass, tearing apart the fighter's outer shell, grinding the flaps, and puncturing the wings.

Brazen could do little but hold on as Cyrus pitched the reconnaissance fighter in a downward spiral in a wild dogfight around the swooping enemy planes.

Justus' white Fokker rushed the F.2A from above once more, cutting across the portside with its guns, and damaging the Vickers gun. The lead Fokker dove steeply, then committed to a tight turn to claw at the F.2A 's horizontal stabilizers.

Acrid smoke bled out of the F.2A 's engine as something gave out with a sputter and screech.

Outnumbered and outgunned, Cyrus descended quickly, hoping to land the craft before it fell apart at the seams or caught flames. The forest canopy directly below was thick, its high branches slapping callously against the landing gear.

"Hang on!" Cyrus said, as he pulled down his aviator goggles to avoid losing his sight to broken lenses.

The F.2A dropped into the forest, slamming into the brush and undergrowth as it arrived at the edge of the woods, then finally struck the ground – lifting dirt high into air as the fighter slewed across the dense glade. The landing gear and part of the wings fell apart on impact, but the F.2A grounded safely on its tarnished ventral side and stopped its oblique impetus with a rough jolt.

Slightly dazed, Brazen was the first to act fast by throwing his gear and rifles down to the ground. He looked to Cyrus, who battled a dizzying headache from a nasty cut on his forehead.

"Out of the cockpit, Walter! Find some cover before they come around!"

The Fokkers were circling about, narrowing down on their position. Cyrus looked up at the sky, now filling with grey clouds, and searched for Justus' monoplane. He pulled off his pilot cap and goggles, and readied his Colt .45. "Where is he?!"

Baron Justus, his Fokker blending against the backdrop, barreled down at a near perpendicular path to the left of the downed fighter. Both Cyrus and Brazen heard the encroaching propeller noise, and were too late to dodge his strafing run as the Baron swept across them with guns blazing.

The bullets scraped Brazen's upper left arm before he jumped out of the plane and onto the grass. Cyrus was hit repeatedly on his torso, and slumped back into his cockpit seat, his head drooping over the edge.

The white Fokker glided past, ascending victoriously.

Brazen, grunting at his grazed arm, stood up and ran to Cyrus. He grabbed the bleeding pilot by his arms, and pulled him down from the cockpit. He dragged him across the ground, spotting one of the Baron's Fokker pilots coming about to finish off the F.2A in a spur of sadism.

"Walter!" Brazen lifted Cyrus up by his collar. "Walter, come on!"

Cyrus' lifeless eyes were open skyward, and there was no breath left in him. Brazen clenched his jaw in sorrow, laying his friend down gently on the grass.

"You still got your wings..." he ushered softly, and took the Colt from Cyrus' hand, and put it away in his equipment belt.

He turned to face the approaching Fokker, his pace steady as he returned to the F.2A. Climbing its broken lower wing strut, he unlocked the gear that pinned down the Lewis aircraft machine gun to the observer's aft seat, and lifted it at the enemy with fearless determination.

The Fokker pilot fired his guns, smashing the ground and throwing dirt into the air – slicing a path toward the fallen reconnaissance fighter.

Brazen, wielding the heavy machine gun with both hands and aware of its frenetic sway, fired its entire load onto the Fokker's engine until the fuel manifold bursted in flames and spewed out of the exhaust pipes. The entire monoplane was ablaze by the time it flew over Brazen, and crashed pitilessly into the woods.

Brazen carelessly dropped the spent machine gun with a clatter, descended from the ruined Bristol fighter, and recovered his gear. Pulling the pin off another grenade, he tossed it into the broken aircraft, and strode away to safety – dragging Cyrus' body with him – before the plane exploded into unrecoverable wedges.

Chapter 12

*T*hunder crackled and rolled as the ravening clouds churned with lightning, and the downpour splashed hardheartedly onto the Landsturm infantrymen waiting on Geist's orders.

The Major-General was perched patiently on his idle motorcycle, the troops standing taut in a row behind him, and the Ottoman Zag mounted on his horse at his side. They watched the sky over the dark forest surrounding the airfield and factories, their trench coats drenched, and finally perceived Baron Justus' Fokker squadron returning to the airfield.

[I count only seven,] Zag noted in Turkic.

In the horizon behind them, past the hard rain, a few pillars of rising smoke could be seen as petrol, timber, and canvas burned.

Geist was disappointed at the disproportionate loss of so many German planes for a single enemy scout. He awaited the Baron's debrief on the dogfight, but required solid proof that the mission directives were accomplished.

[I need a body count,] Geist ordered. [Send out the hunting parties. Go with them.]

Zag acknowledged the command, and turned his horse to face the troops. [Mobilize! Find the survivors, or what's left of them!]

As lightning flashed above them, Daimler Marienfelde transport trucks rolled in, and the assigned infantry embarked onto the three-ton transports. The remainder mounted on trained horses, and flanked the transports.

The gates opened, and Zag led the trucks and cavalry onto the thoroughfare and into the forest, as the monoplanes flew overhead....

With the road awash in sludge, most of the transport trucks had their solid tires and spoked wheels deep in the loam and were unable to advance further. The cavalry, faring no better with exhausted horses, took charge of the expedition, with the Landsturm infantry dividing into squads to cover a larger area in their search for the downed planes. The hunt was made all the more difficult with the forest canopy obscuring the view, and the rain snuffing out the flames from the wrecks.

Annoyed at the slow progress, Zag supervised on horseback as soldiers strained at the chore of pulling one of the trucks from its muddy pit using wooden levers and ropes. The Ottoman kept a keen eye on the dark woods around them, discerning tricks of light and shadow from potential threats.

A movement in the treetops caught his attention, and he swiftly wielded the Gewehr 98 rifle from under his overcoat and fired a single round – startling the soldiers and spooking the horses.

A large, predatory bird came crashing through the branches, and fell onto the brush with its wings spread out and deathly still. It was a common buzzard, its bloody feathers now mingling with the rain and dirt.

Zag grunted, turning to the confused soldiers in his native tongue. [What are you standing around for?! Move that infernal machine out of the muck!] He switched to the Germans' own tongue. [Pull! Pull harder!]

Covered in cowls, a Landsturm squad with stark orders to search on foot trailed each other in single file through the dark, boggy forest. Not knowing they were being watched and followed by Brazen, they battled against the unforgiving vegetation in their path.

The squad's rear-guard used the stock-end his bayonet-studded rifle to climb over a slippery rock, and was a conversationalist amongst the group.

[I heard Oberst Guderian requested a cache of gas bombs from the armory.]

The infantryman ahead of him grumbled as he pulled his foot out of a muddy puddle, nearly losing his boot. [He's loading them on the zeppelin. Says something about townspeople, or the work crew – I don't know, and I don't want to ask.]

The rear-guardsman, unfit for the frontline due to his criminal past when he volunteered, was still curious about the targeted town. [I hope he'll let us raid the place before he uses those damn things.]

The squad leader, a Boer War veteran with a blinded left eye, found the charred remains of an aircraft wing, and alerted the others. [Quiet, all of you! Keep your eyes open for the enemy!]

As the squad advanced, now keeping silent, Brazen emerged from the murk beside the rear-guardsman – slowly removing the push dagger from its sheath. A pace away, he seized the soldier from behind, his dirty hand clasping over the soldier's mouth, and the sharp tip of the dagger pushing its way from the back of the neck until it ruptured through the throat.

The struggling soldier gurgled as blood filled his lungs, dropping his rifle on the wet grass as his hands weakly reached for his neck. Brazen dragged him back into the shadows of the trees before his comrades took notice of his absence.

The remaining Landsturm troopers peered through what was left of the Bristol F.2A, mostly in pieces and a charbroiled skeletal frame. It showed signs it had been a two-seater fighter, and some of the tail markings identified it as either French or British in allegiance, yet the damage was too severe to reveal anything of use to the aircraft engineers.

The shadows between the old trees and the bushes shifted behind them, and the rear-guardsman, the damp hood of his cowl pulled low over his face, rejoined them.

The squad leader, after kicking over a piece of metal, looked over at the cowled man. [You lagged behind to take a piss?]

The rear-guardsman picked up his fallen rifle and pointed to a group of ancient pine trees behind him, the slight changes in his German inflections hidden by the rainfall. [I found them, sir, they're nearby.]

The squad leader drew his suspicions to the knotted trees. [Take point!]

The rear-guardsman promptly led them deeper in the forest to a small grove where a rocky burial mound peered out of the ground. Beneath a cross fastened with branches stripped of leaves, the squad noticed a blistered pilot cap and tarnished goggles on the pile of rocks.

Rifles suddenly rose up to the dark figure leaning at the base of tree beside the mound; his head was drooped low, a Lee-Enfield rifle on his lap.

The squad leader approached Cyrus' body carefully, noting the multiple wounds on the man's torso, and relaxed his aim. [I think we found our enemy agent...] He glanced at the mound. [And his pilot.]

The rear-guardsman bent beside Cyrus, his face still in shadows, and took the rifle. [What do we do now? Should we bury him?]

[Bestow no honor to thine enemies,] a gruff, unkindly Turkic voice replied.

Zag strolled in on his horse, with a company of cavalrymen fanning out behind him, and purposely knocked over the makeshift cross from the mound. He had no respect for those he fought against, those of lesser blood and skewed religion that was not his own, yet he was equally detested back home for not caring who got in his way when he fired his rifle. His bloody stint defending Constantinople and the Gallipoli peninsula in the previous year assured his exile from the Turkish regular army, but serving under Geist only helped to satiate his thrill of the hunt.

Circling the burial mound, Zag would not put it beneath him to desecrate it, but between the muddied trucks, grumbling soldiers, and restless horses, he opted to end this chase.

He looked down at Cyrus' body, then at the squad. [Take the body to the Generalmajor.]

Chapter 13

*I*nside the riveted and welded steel shell of the weapon that was to be known as the tank, dust swirled within the stray light seeping through the open hatch, lighting the cold interior. Tantalus was seated at the driver's station, fervently adjusting the control panel gears to accommodate a bulky portable radio, and was undeterred by the cramped compartment. The caterpillar tracks, two solid chains of steel plates, were yet to be properly installed, and the monstrous powerplant – two 100-horsepower Daimler petrol engines – occupying a good portion of the tank's interior needed extensive calibration to coax far more torque than the specifications allowed.

Junigatsu peered in from the hatchway, her shadow stretched by the light, then crawled inside. "The Germans want their hourly report."

Tantalus was fixated on his chore, for it was the only thing that he felt justified his existence, that made all the trials and tribulations worthwhile, and that he feverishly hoped would immortalize him. "Tell them what I told you on the last report – it's not bloody ready."

"Very well." Junigatsu was numb to Tantalus' cankerous animosity toward authority, as well as his overblown self-worth. "Expect retribution."

"Tell them to send their worst," he answered back dourly.

The tunable SCR-54 radio receiver that Tantalus had appropriated from the Americans via German spies was removed from its wooden shell, and installed with some creative tinkering. Normally used to signal aircraft, a relatively new thing, Tantalus had the foresight of keeping this mechanical behemoth on the forefront of technological advancement. The task had a price in time and patience, both of which were running thin, and his efforts were rewarded with a transient spark from the BC-14 type battery that powered the buzzer circuit that zapped Tantalus' blistered fingers as he accidentally pulled on a copper wire, and he reeled back cursing.

Junigatsu snickered, an unexpected, natural reaction, and he murderously glared at her over his shoulder.

"You want to be useful, little girl?" Tantalus snapped. "What was all that ruckus a while back?"

Junigatsu ignored his tantrum, but appeased his query to indirectly gain his trust without him being consciously aware of it. "A scout plane was intercepted by the Baron's patrols, and shot it down. The Major-General mobilized a detachment of his troops to search the crash site for remains."

"So my countrymen finally found me." Tantalus laughed quietly at his sorry predicament, the proverbial rock and a hard place. "Took them long enough."

"You sound like you want to be found by them." Junigatsu looked at the mad genius from her cursory inspection of the engines and the payload delivery system. "They will just as soon kill you than bring you back under custody."

"Don't you think I know that?" Tantalus snarled, not caring for her patronizing tone. "I just hope that lovely body of yours gets in the way before any harm is brought to me."

"Once your work is finished, I will gladly deliver your head to your former masters myself."

She meant every word, and Tantalus knew it, but he scoffed at her vicious rebuke as she left. He resumed his work now that he was alone, delicately testing the wires jutting out from the panel before him.

"Now..." he said, speaking softly to the machine. "What shall I call you...? How about, *Fenrir*?"

Chapter 14

*T*he rainfall had subsided to a mere drizzle, and the clouds still permeated the firmament. In the company of Colonel Guderian, Geist watched as the hunting parties returned, both the Landsturm infantry and their vehicles drenched and muddied from their trek through the forest.

Zag rode to him proudly, freshly hunted birds and rabbits hanging off his horse's saddle. The excursion, it seemed, had gone well enough that the marksman had time to indulge in his pastimes.

[Back so soon?] Geist said, choosing to pass the Ottoman's transgressions if it meant his mission was a success.

Although Zag was fluent in German, embroiled in his excitement, he replied in Turkic. [I commend the Baron for his brutal efficiency. No one survived.] He turned to the soldiers, realizing that most of the grunts were not as educated in linguistics as the top officers in this outfit. [Bring the body here!]

The troopers unloaded the body they had found near the crash site from the truck at the rear of the column, wrapped in a heavy canvas, and carried him to the Major-General....

*　*　*

Affording from the collective distraction of their grisly prize, as well as the exhaustion of the infantrymen from their ordeal, one of the cowled soldiers discreetly separated from his unit. He headed directly for the factory, keeping to the shadows provided by parked vehicles and equipment crates.

Once inside the armament factory, Brazen discarded the cowl, but kept his Landsturm uniform on. He held the German bayonet-studded rifle at the ready, with the Lee-Enfield rifle strapped to his back.

The tired and angry workers inside the facility paid no attention to him, and remained busy at their tasks as if their lives depended on it. Beyond the chains and struts, Brazen finally saw the mechanical beast that brought him here. Wide treads flanked its chassis, the thick armor studded by an arsenal of weapons both conventional and experimental, but none more terrifying than its main 150mm caliber cannon.

Some of the factory guards manning the catwalks began to notice his unauthorized intrusion, but hesitated to take his threat seriously due to the color of his uniform.

Brazen stayed within the cluttered and shaded areas to avoid being exposed, his eyes searching for Tantalus, and a way to sabotage the operation. There were barrels of kerosene, petrol, grease, and motor oils stored in one corner of the warehouse, and made them potentially flammable given the proper ignition. The barrels would have to be moved to achieve maximum destruction of the tank and the factory, and with so many civilians in the way, the plan was shelved for now.

Brazen moved under the catwalks, and away from the guards' line of sight. He overheard the foreman designating repair orders to a welding crew, referring to a partial blueprint of the tank laid out on a dog-eared worktable near an unfinished, riveted framework component that, when completed and installed, would provide added protection to the tank's rear.

After giving instruction to the welders, the lanky, baggy-eyed foreman folded the drawings, and took them back to his office. Brazen followed him discreetly, and watched him store the papers away inside the steel filing cabinet under lock and key.

Carefully setting the German rifle by the wall inside the office, with the foreman's back still to him, Brazen immediately wrapped the man's neck between the bend of his left arm. Brazen dragged the struggling foreman away from the furniture, constricting the man's throat until he passed out and his body slumped.

Dropping the foreman by the desk, Brazen fished his coveralls for the keys, opened the filing cabinet, and recovered the blueprints. He checked the pockets of his appropriated Landsturm uniform; mixed with spare ammo cartridges and playing cards, he found a small tin case filled with tobacco, a small wooden pipe, and two sets of matches.

Piling everything on the desk, papers, tobacco, and pipe, he lit one set of matches, but kept the second set. The flames grew quickly, starting at one corner and spreading, until blackened flakes shriveled and pulled apart to innumerable jots.

The stolen plans, whether they were copies or originals, were beyond recovery. Picking up the German rifle, Brazen left the office, and closed the door. The smoke from the burning papers melded with the smells of the factory floor, and any noise equally screened by the ruckus of tools and chatter, and none of the guards or workers took notice.

With one objective completed, Brazen now looked to the tank, and the elusive traitor.

From the airfield, leaving his squadron to the care of the mechanics, Baron Justus and two of his pilots approached Geist, as Zag and his contingent of Landsturm infantry presented the operation commander the proof of his kill.

Geist looked down at the face of Cyrus as the soldiers unfurled the canvas, and was insensible to the ashen face of his enemy. [How little difference there is between men and beasts who have fallen on the field.]

Guderian immediately set his tactical mind to work, reflecting on his extensive knowledge of past wars, from ancient times to more recent affairs. [We should send the body back to his superiors. The shock value is worthwhile.]

The suggestion was viable, if not barbaric, but a little human decency was needed to give the soldiers around him a lesson in cautious respect. [Have the soldiers who found him, bury him. Send away any papers addressed to his family, should he have any on his person.]

Guderian was disappointed, but orders were orders.

The Baron arrived just as Geist turned and walked away, and the ace glanced down at Cyrus' corpse. At first befuddled, his memory joggled into clarity, and Baron Justus recognized the pilot he slew.

Guderian noticed the odd reaction. [What is it, Baron? You look like you've just seen a ghost.]

Justus ignored the Colonel, and spun around to Geist's retreating form. [Generalmajor, this is a fraud!]

Geist stopped and looked over his shoulder menacingly. [Fraud?]

Justus pointed at the body, and was careful with his tone. [This is the pilot I shot down this morning! There was another with him, he must be the one you're looking for!]

[Are you absolutely certain, Baron?] Geist demanded, facing the ace fully.

[Yes, sir,] Justus replied confidently, grasping the Major-General despised dishonesty in any form, particularly from his fellow officers. [This isn't the first time I've crossed paths with this pilot; I shot him down in his first sortie before the start of the Marne, and he nearly took me out not long after in a night raid over Verdun.] He bent down to pull away the canvas completely, revealing Cyrus' torn and bloodied uniform. [He wears the patches of a Canadian airman!]

[Impossible,] Zag exclaimed in Turkic. [We found a mound for the pilot beside this man here.]

[Speak a language we can all understand, Ottoman!] Guderian growled in annoyance.

Zag glared at Guderian; his horse shifting nervously. [There were two dead: one was buried, the other lies here.]

Geist's countenance turned deadly serious. [Did you check the mound you spoke of?]

Zag realized his error, and conceded in his native language. [No. I had only assumed.]

Guderian didn't need to translate what Zag had said to know when he was at fault, yet he was impressed by the boldness of their common enemy. [A clever rouse.]

[Sound the alarm!] Geist ordered, setting his army in motion. [Put this facility on alert!]

Chapter 15

*T*he hand-cranked sirens wailed, normally reserved for a disastrous fire or an imminent shelling, and a startling shudder filled the factory for a brief moment before the welders and steel workers abandoned their tools and chores in panic. The four provost guards became duly alert, and descended from the catwalks to contain the situation on the production floor.

Amongst the enveloping consternation, Brazen watched for any sign of the traitor, and spotted Tantalus climbing out of the tank's command hatch. All other priorities faded into the inconsequential, as Brazen locked on to his target with an unflinching gaze.

Tantalus, confused as to the ruckus and cursing at the panic-stricken workmen, instinctively looked past all the cables and girders to the immovable dark figure staring back at him with vicious intensity.

Tantalus, having delved briefly in the shadowy circles of military bureaucracy and retaining an eidetic sensory retention, recognized Brazen. "So," he whispered to himself, "they sent you."

He pointed to Brazen accusingly before death sprung a step. "Intruder!"

The guards reacted, abandoning their task of herding the workers, and focused on the ire of Tantalus' distress. The closest soldier to Brazen, rushed to outflank him, hoping to pin the intruder with the length of his rifle.

Brazen, unshaken by the loss of initiative, pointed his Gewehr 98 at the incoming threat and thrusted its studded bayonet through the German guard's chest. Ripping the pilfered rifle free, Brazen then smashed its hard end against the skull of a second guard attempting to attack from behind. The rifle splintered in half on impact, but effectively disabled the guard that received the blow.

Brazen calmly dropped the broken gun, and pulled out the trench club from his equipment belt before all the wooden shards had fallen safely to the ground. He rushed to the third guard, who hesitated with inexperience and terror to aim his gun at the threat bearing down on him. With the eight-pointed iron ring at the end of the club, Brazen slugged the listless guard, then turned to the last of the henchmen, and sidestepped out of harm's way as the German guard shot a volley – missing Brazen cleanly, but harming a hapless workman. Brazen then quickly closed the distance and clubbed the soldier across the cheek as he attempted to reload.

With five bodies writhing and bleeding on the factory floor, Brazen ran straight for Tantalus, scattering the terrified workmen into a frenzy as they poured out of the building to whatever exit they could find. Tantalus, barely out of the hatch and standing on the tank, was frozen with disbelief at the ease of Brazen's systematic slaughter.

Brazen leapt onto a girder, using it as leverage to land on the tank's capacious track, and just as he brandished the trench club down on the traitor's head, Junigatsu jumped between them and knocked the weapon out of Brazen's hand with a swing of a crowbar – denying the killing blow.

She speared her heel into Brazen's abdomen, and knocked him off the tank. She then turned to Tantalus, ignoring his horrified wails and curses, and unceremoniously shoved him back down the hatch. She threw down the crowbar onto the tank's hull with a resounding metal clang, and gawked over the edge of the track to find Brazen gathering himself from the fall – his fierce eyes locked onto hers....

Locking down the perimeter, the Landsturm infantrymen were scouring the airfield, barracks, and motor pool for infiltrators. Zag, Guderian, and Baron Justus supervised with scrutiny, each fearing blame for this error in judgement, but it was Geist who saw the exodus of frenzied workmen from the main factory.

[The obvious always deludes the proud...] Geist muttered with justifiable acrimony, as this operation escaped his control. [Reform the squads!] he shouted to his scattered soldiers. [Surround the factory!]

Chapter 16

Junigatsu leapt down from the tank, executing a high kick as she landed with cat-like grace. Brazen expertly blocked with his forearm, then again as she delivered another kick to his other flank. He stepped back to widen the distance, but she pressed on with a flurry of fists and elbows.

He parried and dodged each one of her attempts, much to her surprise and frustration. She increased the speed of her next assault, but his reflexes and defensive stance were flawless, until she finally caught the back of his left knee with a low sweep.

Brazen instantly recovered the loss in balance with a backward roll, pedaling away from the reach of her arms or legs. Junigatsu paused her onrush, and couldn't help but feel impressed by his maneuvers.

[You remind me of the old shinobi...] she said to herself. [Are you from the Yagyu or the Iga?]

[Neither one,] Brazen said in her own dialect.

Junigatsu felt exposed, if only briefly. There was more to this intruder than what he let on. [How...? You speak my language just as good as you block my attacks. What are you?]

[You don't need to protect the traitor.]

[No,] Junigatsu agreed in part, [but he's worth something to my benefactors.]

Inside the tank, recovering from his short fall, Tantalus snarled at the pain on his arms, back, and legs as he struggled up. He was all too grateful, or perhaps only fortunate to have avoided a skull fracture.

"Cursed bitch." A toolbox caught his eye, and he quickly dragged it closer. Opening the tin lid, he rummaged through the wrenches, screwdrivers, and hammers for a single-shot Derringer pistol that was no bigger than his hand.

"Can't take away all my toys..."

Junigatsu launched herself at Brazen, driving her kicks at his upper torso, and cornering him against the tank. She then speared her elbow toward his sternum, and Brazen blocked it with the palm of his hand – the sheer force pushing him back.

In that instant, she fetched her knee up onto his groin, sending Brazen bouncing back from the tank hull onto a crouch. She hovered over his penitent and breathless form, content now of having the upper hand.

[Ninjas were nothing more than mystified killers,] she told him. [Glorified thieves, and deified arsonists. I know you've destroyed the designs, but the plans were incomplete when we stole them. The most important bits are in Tantalus' head.]

As she reared back her arm to deliver a debilitating fist on the back of Brazen's skull, he rose up, grabbed hold of the side of her head, and coldly rammed her against the tank's armored skirt.

Stunned, she teetered on her feet for a moment, then fell on her fours.

[I give you this last chance.] Brazen loomed over her. [Walk away.]

Junigatsu looked up at him, her ears ringing and dazed, but her warring spirit was still intact. Removing two tantos from their sheaths she straightened her stance. Brazen, in turn, brandished Cyrus' Colt .45 and pointed it unflinchingly at her forehead.

Behind her, Tantalus climbed down the side of the tank, taking advantage of the deadly distraction to escape.

Brazen adjusted his aim by a degree and fired a round, narrowly missing Junigatsu and purposely scraping Tantalus' shoulder. The traitorous engineer dropped down to his knees, writhing and swearing out of shock than actual pain.

Although Junigatsu was both confused and relieved by the near-miss, she swung her knives at Brazen. He stepped back from the first swing, and blocked the second blade with the sturdy side of his gun.

She continued her thrusts until Geist finally arrived with a contingent of his Landsturm troopers. He was flanked by Guderian and Baron Justus as the soldiers swarmed the production floor and formed lines – drawing their rifles at the intruder.

Now at a severe disadvantage, Brazen switched the Colt from his right hand to his left, then fiercely struck Junigatsu's right wrist with the pistol – knocking the tanto from her grip. He jabbed her trachea with his forearm, then sprinted behind her as she attempted a counter, wrapped his left arm under hers – immobilizing her attempt to strike with her second tanto – and held her still with the Colt's barrel pressing beneath her jaw. Removing the Mauser from its holster with his free right hand, Brazen stretched his arm back and pointed it directly at Tantalus.

He now had two hostages at gunpoint, and the Germans were astonished at his speed and cunning.

Guderian had yet to process what he had just witnessed. [He's no ordinary operative.]

Geist, equally bemused, now knew the face of his adversary. [I wonder if we should risk the lives of our two allies, just so we can see how he expects to escape this bottleneck situation.]

[It will be a fascinating study.] Guderian glanced up at the catwalks. [We should bide our time.]

On the catwalk above them, Zag kept his movements quiet as he readied his long-barreled rifle. With Junigatsu covering Brazen's vital parts, the Ottoman hunter instead aimed for the intruder's exposed right hand, and the Mauser pistol in its grasp.

Geist took a step forward to garner Brazen's staunch gaze. "Are you a friend of Melville?" He taunted at Brazen's brief reaction to a phrase kept only between spies employed by a particularly clandestine sect of British military intelligence.

"Yes, we were warned about you. Otherwise you would have inexorably completed your objectives by now."

Brazen stayed quiet, backing away a few steps knowing there was a sniper somewhere above him.

Tantalus, hurt and unnerved, wavered under the pressure of having a gun pointed at his head. "Shoot him already, Geist! Or let the whole lot of us go!"

"Is that what you want, Herr Tantalus?" Geist challenged, sensing the perturbed engineer was hiding something. "Do you rather take your chances with this devil than with us?"

"At least he's a devil I know," Tantalus replied.

Brazen, without looking down at him, cocked back the Mauser's hammer with an audible unyielding click – startling Tantalus.

Geist regarded both men with suspicion, yet wondered secretly at their past connection. "Go ahead," he goaded, "we can finish the tank without the esteemed engineer."

Brazen, looking straight in the Major-General's eyes, wasn't swayed in the least. "You need him."

The stand-off caused some itchy trigger-fingers amongst the rank-and-file, yet none of these soldiers dared to act without direct orders. Tantalus, finding a glimmer of courage, slowly wrapped his hand around the Derringer concealed in his shirt sleeve.

Tired of speaking the intruder's language, Geist resisted the urge to flinch up at Zag for risk of ruining the Ottoman's upper hand. [How long can we hold this charade? You decide.]

Junigatsu knew a few ways to extricate herself from Brazen's taut muscles pinning her as his human shield, but at the risk of unsettling a rain of bullets. [Surrender,] she whispered in her dialect, [it's your only option.]

[Is this the measure of your duties to the Emperor?] Brazen responded softly, though his words were harsh. [To die on a whim by my hand or by theirs, having accomplished nothing except the means of your demise?]

[Don't be so quick to judge me,] Junigatsu stung back. [You're a nail that's sticking out farther than you should be.]

"I'm not the nail, I'm the sledgehammer."

Guderian, carefully watching the verbal interplay between the intruder and Japanese agent, leaned closer to Geist. [Give the order, Generalmajor.]

[Not yet...] Geist said, eyeing the engineer.

Tantalus, his back against the tank and well within Brazen's shadow, aimed the small gun at the blight in his path to greatness. "And the wolf wakes to the sound of Ragnarok!"

He fired the Derringer's single bullet, striking Junigatsu on her side. On cue, Zag fired a precision round, shooting the Mauser pistol off Brazen's hand with a high-pitched glint. The pistol misfired as it clattered to the floor, ricocheting off the tank armor, and narrowly missing Tantalus by inches.

Brazen's reaction was superhuman. He snatched Junigatsu as she folded, driving his heel at Tantalus and onto the tank's track wheels – knocking the turncoat cold. He shot high with the Colt, piercing Zag's leg and causing the Ottoman to stumble. With his right hand unexpectedly free of the Mauser, he grabbed the last grenade from his belt and pulled the pin with his thumb before the Landsturm could fire their weapons.

Brazen tossed it at Geist and his troops, and moved away quickly.

Knowing too well the carnage a grenade in closed confines could cause, especially with flammable materials lying about, Geist pushed his men back. [Scatter!]

Geist and the Landsturm broke their formation and ran in all directions. After three bounces off the floor, the grenade exploded – blowing a hole through the factory wall.

Shielded from the concussive blast by the tank's armor, and carrying Junigatsu over his shoulder, Brazen dashed through the serrated opening using smoke and consternation to screen his escape.

Out on the field, spotting Zag's startled horse nearby, and with the Landsturm reserve detachment amidst leaderless confusion, Brazen secured Junigatsu onto the steed's back and climbed onto the saddle.

Wrestling with the reins and the horse's reluctance, he spurred the powerful animal to a mad sprint across the airfield and into the surrounding forest.

Chapter 17

Geist's ears were ringing from the explosion, and aside from a few bruises, he was unharmed. A few of his Landsturm infantrymen laid dead or in pieces on the ground, with twice as many wounded. Guderian and Baron Justus were largely spared the shock of the grenade explosion after shielding their bodies behind a stack of steel girders, and were physically unscathed.

[Find him!] Geist commanded, peering through the acrid mist at the officers.

The Baron, eager for battle, was the first out the hole, leading a few able soldiers with him. Guderian held himself against a support beam, one hand rubbing his throbbing temple. Although he had suffered no injury, the noise of the blast painfully overloaded his sensitive hearing.

[The madman will try and delude us in the woods,] Guderian surmised. [We need to burn him out.]

[You're the master tactician, Oberst,] Geist said, as he assisted a staggered trooper to his feet, [take whatever liberties you need.]

Guderian, despite his headache, grinned with morbid callousness, then headed out with renewed vigor.

Geist walked toward the tank, examining it for damage, and was reassured the machine was still intact. Beside him, Zag descended the stairway from the catwalks, limping angrily on a hurt leg while balancing his weight on his rifle.

Geist turned to a soldier, and urged him toward the Turkish hunter. [Take the Ottoman to the infirmary!]

Returning his attention to the armored vehicle, he looked down at Tantalus writhing on the floor. He clutched the dazed engineer by his wounded arm, lifted him up, and shoved him hard against the tank's bulk.

"You're either a lousy marksman, or intentionally stupid."

Tantalus laughed with the throbbing pain from his arm rushing throughout his body, and showed Geist the smoking barrel of the small Derringer. "Now I can finish my work without further distraction."

Zag's well-trained horse raced through the thick German forest under Brazen's steady command, carrying him and the incapacitated Junigatsu on its muscular back and deeper into the woods.

The Imperial agent moaned from the bullet wound at her side, and the sheer discomfort kept her eyes closed as she pressed her head on Brazen's chest. He held on to her tightly, a hand putting pressure on the wound in the hope of stemming back the blood loss, while the other steered the reins.

Somewhere above him, the crimson and waxen shapes of the Baron's Fokkers could be seen through the leafy canopy, flying low and slow in an attempt to stalk them....

Baron Justus maneuvered his white fighter through the loose formation of his remaining squadron, and led them to lower heights and speed. Through the thick leaves of the treetops, he could see the blurry shape of Zag's horse galloping hard on an uneven path, appearing and disappearing under the brush and branches.

He could faintly see Brazen holding on to Junigatsu, wounded but alive, then turned to his pilots and signaled for them to attack. One by one, the Fokker monoplanes broke formation, tipping on their port wings and diving as low as their machines allowed without the engine stalling midflight. Amassing enough airspeed to stay afloat and to catch up to their ground target, they opened fire with their onboard guns.

Bullets meant to destroy aircraft zipped through the woods, violently scattering leaves, ripping branches with ease, and thrashing through the bark of age-old trunks – spitting wooden splinters into the air.

Brazen steered the horse away from the swathe of destruction that crept up from behind. Dirt and grass kicked up as the Fokkers committed their strafing runs, but were each unable to score a direct hit. One by one, the planes veered off in wide arcs to attempt another pass.

Brazen saw the path ahead, although never keeping a straight line as gunfire ripped the ground around him, and he was unable to stop the horse's impetus, as it took them into a clearing. He spurred the horse harder, discerning the Fokker pilots now had an unobstructed view of their target and plenty of space to aim their guns.

Three of the crimson monoplanes caught up, and in single file, they flew close to the ground to fire their weapons – their landing gears forcefully parting the tall grass. The verdant clearing tore apart from the barrage, but the horse, accustomed to war, was unshaken.

With the edge of the forest encroaching faster than the Fokkers, Brazen hugged Junigatsu and ducked a series of low-lying branches as the horse took them back into the cluttered safety of the old woods.

The Fokkers, caught up in the euphoria of their savagery, immediately abandoned their blitzing and pulled back hard on their ailerons to gain altitude. Two of the three safely arced out of the forest's entangled embrace, while the last of the trio crashed into the treetops.

The monoplane's wings and fuselage ripped apart, but the pilot miraculously survived, albeit remorselessly ejected from hls seat.

This was no relief to the Baron as his white fighter flew by, and he scowled at the loss of yet another plane as the rest of the Fokker squadron resumed formation astern. Hearing the familiar drone of an airship, he decided to break away from the pursuit and fell back, flying around the massive form of the zeppelin above them, and reforming at its flanks as escorts.

* * *

In the zeppelin's control car, Guderian studiously scoured the forest with a pair of binoculars at the navigator's window as the airship pilots maneuvered the versatile craft. Gunners were at their station above the forward hull, manning a pair of Parabellum machine guns on free mountings, ready to fire on command while the bomb doors opened.

[Increase speed!] Guderian ordered, lowering his binoculars. [Release the payload!]

Dozens of mortars and bombs dropped from the zeppelin's racks, exploding as they hit the ground, and leaving a blossoming trail of fire along its wake. The trees and underbrush were instantly incinerated by the rolling wildfire, and the charred remains pushed aside by the shockwave of each explosion.

The fiery glow of the destruction fleetingly reflected on his cheeks as Guderian scrutinized over the blackened scraps of the timberland, and what he hoped, the burnt bones of the enemy. The intense heat of the fires reached them, causing enough turbulence in the airways that the pilots had to adjust their pitch.

[All bombs have been spent, Oberst, minus the special canisters,] the navigation officer reported. [Orders?]

Guderian mulled in thought. [If there's a chance he survived, where could he run to resupply...?] The odds of anything surviving the blaze below were slim, but he understood the strategic benefit of overestimating his enemy, especially an agent who deluded a sadistic hunter like Zag.

[Orders, sir?] the officer insisted uneasily.

Guderian killed the smile that crept up on his lips as he imagined a proper solution to the Major-General's problem. [Signal Baron Justus to return to base, then turn this ship around to rendezvous with our ground troops.]

Hot ash and embers rained down on Brazen, and he could feel the heat surround him and Junigatsu like a constricting blanket. Thick, black smoke choked the sky, obscuring them from unfriendly eyes, and by mere luck he reached his destination. Not far from where he and Cyrus had crash-landed, there was an abandoned bear cave, and he forced the horse headlong through its maw and the safety of its earthly walls.

Deep in the cave, where he had stashed most of his gear after the plane crash, Brazen quickly dismounted from the horse and carefully carried Junigatsu to the farthest corner. He ripped open her blood-stained shirt and checked her injury. She bled, and to her fortune the bullet had gone straight through.

Outside, whiffs of smoke and falling cinders covered what was left of the forest after the firestorm. Looking longingly to the cave's entrance, Zag's horse shuffled nervously on its hooves.

Reaching into his gear for the medic's kit he had appropriated from Cyrus' downed fighter, Brazen looked up at the horse. "You've taken us as far as you can. Return to your master."

Hesitant, the horse neighed at Brazen, then galloped away in haste.

He unpacked the field blanket from his backpack, and wrapped it behind Junigatsu's head, then grabbing a debridement tool, a bottle of liquid antiseptic, and dressing from the wooden kit, Brazen tended to the wound at her side.

Chapter 18

*T*he bullet holes and pitted gashes of the armament factory's walls were being hastily patched, while the blood, oil, and grease stains were washed away with water, soap, and a good scrub.

Geist was standing tall on the steel titan, observing the welders and steel workers involved in the repairs. With the tank virtually constructed, leeway was allowed for the work crew to retire for the night under the watchful eye of the Landsturm infantrymen. There was a need to be vigilant should the civilians attempt to escape out of fear of being targeted by a more concerted Allied attack, or perhaps emboldened by the actions of the enemy saboteur to revolt altogether. The workers' sheer numbers would overwhelm the Landsturm forces – guns, or no guns.

The Major-General glanced down the gaping hole of the open hatchway, and descended into the cramped space occupied largely by the brutish power plant, gun belt feeds and munitions loading apparatuses. Too tall to stand inside, Geist reserved the awkwardness of slouching, and sat on the main cannon's turret base while one foot hung onto the short ladder rung by the hatch for balance.

Tantalus was sitting in the commander's chair, making careful adjustments to the instrumentation under the light of lanterns.

"I want this beast rolling on its tracks by the first light of morning," Geist said.

Tantalus kept at his task. "All that Fenrir requires is the live ordnance for its main cannon, but otherwise it's ready for your test run, Generalmajor. It has been for a while."

Geist frowned at that final statement. "I don't appreciate the duplicity, Herr Tantalus."

"The workers fear for their lives," Tantalus replied without an ounce of concern for the German's officer's displeasure, "as they believe they're expendable to preserve this project's secrecy. So they find little things to keep themselves preoccupied, and alive for a little longer."

"*You* seem preoccupied."

Tantalus snorted with a sound of a man who considered himself intellectually superior to anyone German, British, or otherwise. "Minor calibrations. Unless you want this thing to stall over a ditch."

Clicking his tongue at the engineer's condescending deportment, Geist decided to challenge the traitor's conviction. "From what I've gathered, Herr Tantalus, you and the saboteur have a history."

Tantalus let out a humorless laugh. "Hardly," he said without looking back at the Landsturm commander, as he tested the engaging mechanisms of the gated gear shifters. "I ran into him a while back when the Landships Committee initiated the

Gauntlet venture alongside the Little Willie project. While the prototype of what would become the tank was given to the Navy, the Gauntlet was given to the private sector to build."

Geist recalled the accounts given by Junigatsu, and seconded by the German spy network.

"Although the side-project was manned by civilian engineers," Tantalus continued, "it was overseen by Military Intelligence... Brazen, as he's called, was one of them."

"As were you."

Tantalus briefly leered over his shoulder at the Major-General. "I was a 'friend of Melville', yes, but not an operative. I was a record keeper with a degree that proved useful in the chief design and construction of the parallel prototype..." He snarled to himself at the failures that were forced on him by his British kinsmen. "Though those bastards rejected almost all of my ideas to supplement what was already an indestructible shell. But—"

He patted the control board, eager to wake Fenrir. "I never quite thanked you for allowing me my creative freedom in finishing what I started."

"Thank the Kaiser," Geist said. "My opinion of you is far more discriminating."

Tantalus shared the lack of trust between them, but at least they had a common foe that united them in their efforts. "Regardless, what I currently know of Brazen is from what I've studied from his file – at least that which I had access to. He's a professional who's had successful operations in every corner of the world: surveillance in Japan and the States;

propaganda in France and Canada; sabotage in Russia, and assassinations in England, South Africa, and New Zealand."

"To think such valiant men are kept in the shadows." Geist was impressed, with the saboteur's name now fitting the man's reputation. "What do you know of his personal life?"

"Anything that can prove useful? Nothing. Born in the Atlantic as a subject of the British Commonwealth, with an Irish mother and a father who was a member of the littoral merchant fleet. Lived sporadically throughout the Empire until his father's death, then settled in Japan with his mother until she passed away. He joined the Canadian Legion of Frontiersmen at the age of fifteen; stationed as a special constable in London in 1909, then drafted to the Secret Service bureau three years later."

"Your memory is hardly laggard."

"It helps to know the face of your killer."

Geist's distrust was ever more prevalent. "You suspected it would be this Brazen to come for your head?"

Tantalus nodded. "A guess that's morbidly accurate, as will be my confidence in this tank's success on the field."

"By all means, Herr Tantalus. Our wholesome victory hinges on your confidence."

Chapter 19

Junigatsu's waking moan stopped Brazen's contemplative writing, and he glanced over at her as she struggled to regain her bearings inside the dank bear cave with the smell of burnt timber sifting through the opening. He put away his journal, all his gear and weapons safely beside him should she react as a willing enemy.

Wondering why her shirt was torn, and a bullet-ridden flight jacket covered her shoulders, Junigatsu winced in pain as she propped herself up against the cave wall. It had been a long time since she had felt this way, sore and physically depleted, and it reminded her of her arduous training, which was all the more painful as a woman in a society that considered her gender second-class. Those trials had broken many, but she persevered, and that pride empowered her.

She checked the bandages wrapped around her waist and abdomen, then finally became aware of Brazen's austere presence with a slight startle.

"The bullet passed through you," Brazen said, "so you should recover. It missed your spleen by an inch..." He felt her hostility and confusion, but nothing malevolent.

[I don't know why I saved you,] he told her in her language, [but I did.]

Junigatsu was at a disadvantage in her state, yet despite the situation, she strangely did not feel threatened. [You must have a reason. If you would've left me, the Germans would have taken care of me.]

Brazen doubted it. "Would they? Or would they've taken the opportunity to relieve their shoulders of a minor burden?" He took a canteen from his gear, hearing the cooled water within its tin shell slosh about. "From the reports that I read before I was deployed, Japan had annexed some Micronesian colonies and a coaling port from the Germans. Hardly the actions of allies."

He tossed her the canteen, and she caught it at the cost of a throbbing twinge below her ribs. She gritted her teeth together, exhaled slowly, and let the ache fade. "There was never an alliance. This is strictly an enterprise."

She opened the cap, sniffed it for good measure, and gingerly drank the water from the canteen. She would normally be grateful, but she remained suspicious, and instead looked outside to the piles of cinders and mounds of ash that was once a woodland. She was saddened by such loss, and realized just how far the Germans were willing to go to achieve their aims.

"Why did Tantalus shoot you?" Brazen asked, intending to gauge where she stood in the hierarchy of the German operation.

Junigatsu grimaced at the name. "He missed you, and hit me."

[You sound doubtful,] he said in Japanese.

[I am...] she admitted plainly. [What will you do with me now?]

"You will need at least three days to convalesce. What you decide to do with yourself is obviously up to you." Brazen stood up and gathered his gear. "I've left you enough water and rations, and a knife that belonged to the man whose uniform I briefly borrowed."

He grabbed the Lee-Enfield rifle leaning on the wall, fitted with a battle-worn scope, and prepared to leave the cave.

Junigatsu looked over at the supplies that were left behind, and deliberated rushing for the knife, but it was too far out of reach – purposely so. [What's your name?]

"Brazen."

"I'm Junigatsu."

Brazen peered back over his shoulder and grinned warmly. "December... that was the month I left Japan."

He walked away, leaving Junigatsu to fend for herself. Looking down at the spot where he had stashed his gear, she discovered a timeworn, leather-bound book. With a demanding physical exertion that left her nearly breathless, she crawled over and picked up the journal. Once the pain subsided, she flipped through its delicate hand-written pages, and was surprised that most of the text was written in both English and Japanese. An old photograph slipped out, its edges torn, and it showed a Japanese family in pose, with a young boy that resembled Brazen standing close to an elderly, but stately matriarch and her daughters. Attached with a rusty clip behind the family photo were the oval locket portraits of a man and woman of Commonwealth descent whose facial features were shared by Brazen.

Appreciating, with some puzzlement as to why, that Brazen had left this behind for her to find, Junigatsu looked to the cave entrance only to find him gone.

The golden hues of a new dawn washed over the airfield, stretching the shadows of the hangars and factories, and the quiet serenity was dreadfully disturbed by the mechanized rumbling of the Fenrir tank prototype treading across the terrain at furious speeds. Its rolling tracks kicked up plumes of dust and pieces of earth in its wake, and left grinding skid marks as it suddenly pitched to the side and glided across the dew-stricken ground in a sharp turn.

It slid to a halt, and its main cannon set to motion as it chased an unseen target in a full 360 degree rotation and 45 degree elevation. It pivoted back to the front, where Geist, Baron Justus, and a few awestruck Landsturm officers watched the nascent of a weapon twenty years ahead of its time, and far unlike anything that had been deployed by the Allies thus far into the Great War.

The command hatch opened, and Tantalus – dressed in dirty dust goggles and leather helmet – climbed out with well-earned pride at his work. He was able to operate the tank alone for this demonstration, but a proper crew that included a loader, gunner, and mechanic would maximize the weapon's effectiveness in combat.

"Just as I told you, Major-General!" Tantalus cried out enthusiastically.

Geist nodded approvingly. "Very good, Herr Tantalus. While you begin training a tank crew, I will get the Kaiser's blessings to begin mass production."

[Most impressive,] Justus said, standing at Geist's side. [We may yet beat out the other manufacturers with this revolutionary design. I've seen the preliminaries of the Sturmpanzerwagen from Daimler, and although imposing, it looks awkward at best. Even the Brits are churning out advanced variations of their tank since the Somme, but nothing like this monster.]

[A lucrative and exclusive contract does sound enticing, Baron, if you're willing to step down from your fighter and start running the factory.] Geist respected the ace pilot for his professionalism, but still detested his overly social habit of talking far more than was necessary. [Where's the Oberst?]

[Still out on the prowl,] Justus answered.

Putting on his gloves, Geist walked to his parked motorcycle. [Send the Ottoman to fetch him back. We got business to take care of here.]

Kick-starting the bike, and pulling back on the throttle, Geist rode away.

Zag, his leg wound bandaged tightly, was leaning on his long-barreled rifle as he caressed his horse's cheek and brow.

Discharging himself from the sick berth against the German doctor's advice, he had started his rounds along the perimeter of the factory grounds when his mount found its way back to him.

[I'm disappointed that you allowed yourself to be spirited by an infidel,] Zag whispered softly to his horse in Turkic, [but I'm glad you returned to me. You're a good steed, a blessed gift from my oldest brother.]

He patted the horse's neck as it snorted in response, affectionately singing a soothing lullaby from the days long gone, then brushed away the bits of dried leaves and wooden splinters from his horse's long mane. [It didn't take long to tame you, but you're still stubborn.]

Behind him, a Landsturm officer approached, and saluted, despite the gesture's uselessness, and looked to the Ottoman and his horse nervously.

[I have orders from Generalmajor Geist, sir.]

Zag started to remove the horse's saddle and restraints. [I know,] he replied in German without acknowledging the officer's presence. [I will be departing to meet with Guderian soon.]

He tossed the dusty saddle and reins to the officer, who caught the heavy load by surprise.

[I set you free, my friend,] Zag said to the horse in Turkic. [Away with you.]

He slapped the horse's hind, startling it to a gallop. He watched its harmonious gracefulness as it treaded across the field with deep admiration, then raised his rifle, pulled back its lever, and aimed its cold barrel at the horse.

He shot it at a distance, and watched the equine beast collapse heavily on its forward momentum.

Zag turned to the startled officer, switching to the local tongue. [Fetch me a new horse.]

Chapter 20

*B*razen climbed over a decrepit picket fence, flakes of white paint shaking free like autumn leaves, and landed quietly into the clutter of abandoned farm equipment that surrounded a storage building at the edge of the village. Situated on the outskirts of the forest, it was far from Stuttgart, and about three hours from the armament factory, and he suspected the majority of the workers were drawn from this quaint farming community that lacked a proper name from the army maps he had studied. He avoided the main road, which was nothing less of a muddy path that ran through the entirety of the village, and obscured his movements by moving from the shadow of one obstacle to another.

Crossing the gate of another fence, he was becoming aware of the suspicious lack of inhabitants and farming activity even at this early hour, and his senses flared on full alert when he spotted a dead German Sheperd lying halfway inside an open barn.

Its eyes were wide and bloodshot, with a blue tongue peeking between its lips, as if it had asphyxiated to death. Looking past the animal, Brazen saw the bodies of a few cattle and villagers sprawled inside the barn, and all had died the same agonizing way. There was also a hole in the roof where a canister shell was dropped, and detonated within.

Brazen quickly pulled out the rudimentary gas mask and small-box respirator from his satchel, and strapped it tightly over his face and neck. He had witnessed the gruesome effects of chlorine gas on the French-Algerian troops at Ypres the year prior; watched brave men coughing and sneezing uncontrollably as their lungs collapsed like shriveled leather gloves, with blisters braking out on exposed skin, and anyone who survived the confusion were blinded for life.

Given adequate motivation and funding, humanity's imaginative capacity for mass murder had no bounds. A gun, at least, was merciful by comparison.

He entered the shed attached to the barn to check for any other victims, but found it unoccupied. It was filled with a variety of tools. from saws, plows, hammers, prongs, and shovels. Lifting a burlap sack of a small crate nestled under a pickaxe and hand drill, Brazen found several bundles of dynamite. He guessed the farmers used them to uproot old tree stumps and boulders to clear the way for more farmland, and kept them free from dampness and anything flammable.

The bundles were small enough to fit in his backpack, and seeing that the dead villagers no longer had a use for them, he promised to repay them the only way he knew how.

The clanking and racketing of motors and wheels racing out of the forest drew Brazen back outside. Just as he swung out his Lee-Enfield rifle to the ready, a convoy of Daimler Marienfelde transport trucks broke through the fences, carrying an entire platoon of Landsturm assault troopers. The vehicles formed an enclosure, unloading the soldiers before braking to a stop.

Brazen shot the first two soldiers that landed their boots on the ground, but all else trampled over their mangled bodies to surround him. None of the troopers fired back, perhaps given orders to take him alive, or were trained well enough to be mindful of accidentally shooting each other.

A heavyset trooper dropped behind Brazen, wresting the rifle from his hands. Brazen let go of the rifle, and delivered a high elbow under the man's jaw – driving the man's teeth into his tongue. He pulled out his push dagger, and stabbed the next soldier to rush him, planting the blade deep in the abdomen. Pulling the dagger out, he then stabbed a second trooper in the upper leg. He pivoted fast, and slashed yet another infantryman across the nose and brow before the swarm of aggravated soldiers overran him like players in a vicious rugby match.

In the scuffle, his mask was knocked away, and he lost grip of his dagger's bloodied hilt; it slipped out of reach as a soldier inadvertently kicked it into the mud. The soldiers pounded on Brazen, kicked him, then locked his limbs with their combined weight, until he was finally on his knees.

They forcibly unstrapped his gear and brutishly disarmed him, then pulled back from him quickly as the rest of the Landsturm troopers encircled the stooped Brazen with bayonet-studded rifles pointed and ready. The soldiers were shoulder to shoulder, leaving no gap, and slowly encroached on his position with carefully-measured half-steps.

Disoriented from the beating, panting from the kicks to his ribs, Brazen looked up at his aggressors with an eagerness to continue fighting. Blood trickled down from a split lower lip, turning to droplets over his chin, and the soldiers smartly kept their distance.

[Your stealth has been compromised.] A gap opened in the circle of guns and wits, and Colonel Guderian stepped forward with relative calm and arrogance. Behind him, the zeppelin soared out of the forest and over the tops of the buildings. [You have little option but to submit.]

Brazen recognized him as an officer, but not of this division of the Home Guard. [You gassed these people?]

Guderian held back his surprise at Brazen's flawless German. [They were... uncooperative in helping us to arrange this trap for you. Deep in your enemy's lands, where else would you resupply?]

The Colonel sighed, feigning remorse at murdering innocent civilians for the sake of keeping his objectives. [But, not to worry, we are safe from harm.] He offered Brazen a smirk promising far worse than a demise by chemical exposure. "For you, just for a little while."

Brazen found the push dagger half-buried in the mud between him and Guderian, but the Colonel noticed it also and fished it out. He studied the dirty blade curiously, then blindly gave it to a soldier behind him to confiscate with the rest of the equipment. Yet the Colonel sensed a ruse, and suspected Brazen had been eying the bodies of the troopers lying in the dirt with their guns and tools dangling from their belts ripe for the taking.

[Remove these bodies, quickly,] Guderian commanded, staring at Brazen to measure his reaction, but the man was as unreadable as a stone wall. [Although I am most impressed by your skill and guile,] Guderian said, as the dead soldiers were carried away. [I wonder about your endurance...]

He scoffed with twisted amusement, and motioned to the troopers behind Brazen. The select group, their loyalties bought and paid for to serve the Colonel, slung their rifles over their shoulders, wrapped a canvas belt around Brazen's neck to mute his resistance, and pinned his legs and arms down, while they tied his wrists together with rope, then unceremoniously dragged him over to the village square halfway across the main street.

The Landsturm troopers, some seeking vengeance for their lost brethren, others out of vehemence, threw Brazen by the well, enclosed with wooden boards to keep the rainfall out, and delivered their cruelty with bare knuckles. Brazen conserved his energy, and absorbed the abuse, even as they strung him up by his wrists until his feet dangled defenselessly over the covered shaft. The tallest of the bruisers acted as an interrogator, but received no answers from Brazen.

Guderian watched, pacing placidly before the grilling, while around them, the troops were pilfering the village for unspoiled food and valuables and loading them on the trucks.

Seeing Brazen's gear near his path, carelessly abandoned by one of the officers to partake in the raid, he bent down to pick up a curious weapon hidden cleverly behind the backpack: a sheathed Japanese sword. He lifted it high with a gloved hand, while the other remained at the small of his back, and studied at the ornate family crest on the lacquered scabbard.

He pulled out the sword partway, mindful of its sharpness, and he was surprised at its shortness, though what remained at the tip glinted as dangerously as its razor-like edge.

[A broken blade...?] Guderian wondered to himself why the saboteur would keep such an outdated weapon, and a faulty one at that. What is a sword against a machine gun these militant days, or against a full range of artillery, but a sentimental placard of an age long gone?

His fascination lasted briefly, as he slid the blade back in place, then discarded it. Growing bored, he stifled a yawn, and was almost glad to see the Ottoman Zag arrive on a new horse astride a coterie of four cavalrymen.

[Ah, Ottoman, what news do you bring? Did our grand landship survive its first trial?]

Zag was unmoved by the dead villagers and rampant looting by Guderian's men. [It did, and Generalmajor Geist demands your presence there.]

[All the better,] Guderian said. [My part in this little affair is done.]

Zag looked to Brazen, recognizing the operative who shot his leg and stole his horse. [You caught the devil...] he muttered in Turkic, then realized the Colonel caught none of his words. [What have you learned from him?]

[Surprisingly nothing,] Guderian said. [Not a word, nor a scream, and his blood is the only thing that proves he's human.] He glowered at Brazen with disappointment while addressing the soldiers reveling in their mistreatment of the prisoner. [Cease! This exercise in civility is proving useless.]

The soldiers beating on Brazen back away, tired, and joined the rest of the troops loading the trucks in preparation to leave town, allowing Zag and his cavalrymen to approach the well.

[He's yours to do as you please,] Guderian told Zag, and as an afterthought, he gestured at Brazen's belongings. [You can have his gear as a trophy.]

[His head will do fine, Oberst.]

[Whatever pleases you, Ottoman, but this time show proof that you committed the deed,] Guderian derided, much to Zag's vexation, then turned to the assault troopers. [Gentlemen, we depart now!]

Guderian left with his entourage, as Zag pompously circled around Brazen like a vulture to a carcass. The encumbered trucks moved out of the village, some struggling with the uneven road.

[What shall I do with you?] Zag asked Brazen in Turkic. [Give you a merciful death?]

Bruised and bleeding, Brazen kept his head drooped.

[You tested my pride when you shot me, and you forced my hand when you stole my good horse,] the Ottoman hunter vented, well aware that the cavalrymen couldn't understand his guttural frustrations. [What mercy do I owe you, except that which Allah has already prepared?]

Zag pointed to one of the cavalrymen, his anger simmering to the surface. [Cut him down!]

One of the equestrian soldiers complied by unsheathing his curved cavalry saber, and slashing the rope with a clean stroke – freeing Brazen. He collapsed to his knees, then onto his side, his wrists still in binds.

Zag snappishly waved his hands, becoming increasingly impatient. [Bring him to his knees!]

Three of the cavalrymen dismounted with pistols drawn, and brusquely dragged Brazen to his knees. Fatigued, he offered no resistance, and kept his head down.

With some strain on his bandaged leg, Zag got off his horse and approached. He saw the nape of Brazen's neck, and removed his infantry issue saber from its steel scabbard. Still not content, he viciously grabbed Brazen's jaw and forced him to meet face to face.

Zag's spittle flew with his Turkic curse. [Live like an animal, die like one!]

Pushing Brazen's head away, Zag reared back and raised his saber high over his head with both hands on the hilt. The cavalrymen backed away fearfully, then in an instant, Brazen reared up and batted Zag under the jaw with his bound fists and all his might.

The attack knocked spit, blood, and teeth from Zag, as he bent backward at a sharp angle from the impact – the lambswool colpack tumbling away from his head. Zag's hands let go of the saber, and Brazen caught it in midair, then circled around and cut down the nearest cavalryman.

He charged the next confounded soldier, as he let off a wild shot from his handgun, and slashed him from shoulder to side, before finishing the third dismounted cavalier by garroting him.

The fourth cavalryman spurred his horse in an attempt to mow down the enemy, but Brazen stepped aside and dropped low to cut across the horse's legs. As the beast faltered, the cavalryman was catapulted from his saddle, and crashed headlong into the dirt.

Brazen ran up behind him, and hammered the saber onto the man's exposed back.

He turned to the Ottoman, who was struggling to contain his pain with a broken jaw. Walking the last few steps, Brazen thrusted the entire length of the saber's blade through Zag's chest. Zag gasped in shock, and fell back – the peering blade at his back impaling itself into the ground. Zag slipped onto it until his shoulder hit the mud, and the bloody saber now stuck out from his chest.

Brazen severed his bonds on the edge of the impaled sword, and looked around for his gear and the parting troop convoy. Beyond still, hovering toward the direction of the armament factory, was the woeful zeppelin.

Ignoring his need to rest and lick his wounds, he gathered his katana and what was left of his equipment, then sprinted after the convoy.

Chapter 21

*T*rucks carrying train parts and metal sheets rolled into the warehouse docks where Landsturm soldiers assisted in unloading and transferring the supplies with cranes and carts in preparation to connect rail tracks from the factory depot to the main train line a short distance away. Geist oversaw the operation while he waited for Guderian's arrival. Now that they had a working prototype of their advanced weapon, they needed the blessings from the Kaiser's General Staff, and a proper manufacturing firm with skilled tradesmen to begin rolling out the machines before the Americans decided neutrality was no longer in their best interests.

This facility was compromised, and the indentured workers along with it. A small sacrifice was needed to be made for greater gains.

A commotion stirred behind him, and he turned to see a Landsturm patrolman and a medic assisting Junigatsu across the airfield toward him. Despite her weakened condition, she frustrated the medic's efforts to inspect her bandages.

Geist faced her, quietly surprised. "Fortune smiles on you, my dear. Let the medic see your wound."

With reluctance, she allowed the medic to check her side. "The saboteur treated me, then left once I awoke."

[Did he now?] Geist found it odd, though the woman was a temporary ally, he did not doubt her. "He wanted nothing else?"

She winced as the medic's probing left no grace as to his skills. "I'm not sure he knew himself what his intentions were, other than using me as a human shield." She offered Geist Brazen's journal. "He left this behind."

Geist took the book, and flipped through its worn pages with earnest intrigue, stopping at a hand-drawn diagram of a katana and all its constituent parts written in Japanese scrawl.

[Curious...]

"It's either a record of his life," Junigatsu surmised, as she pushed the medic away from her, "or a story of someone else's."

"An insight to his thoughts perhaps?" In the skies past Junigatsu, he saw the approaching zeppelin. [The Oberst's finally here.] He closed the book, but kept it close. "Perhaps you should rest before you assume your duties. Tantalus has become rather wild as of late."

"Where is he?"

Geist sensed her dread, and understood it. "Fine-tuning his so-called wolf."

Alone with the tank in the dark and spacious interior of the factory, Tantalus adjusted the last of the bolts on a side panel. His mind was entirely on gears and pistons, future improvements to streamline assembly, when a shadow crossed the sliver of sunlight peering from the rafters behind him.

Frightful, he glanced back, and his eyes widened at the sight of his Japanese guardian – much to his dismay. "I... I commend your fortitude." He cleared his throat to rid of any lingering fear at her reprisal. "As you can see, the prototype was a complete success."

He patted the tank, then looked to her while avoiding the fierce anger in her dark brown eyes. He noticed the bandages around her lower torso, and quietly scolded himself for his poor marksmanship. "I suppose, despite all gestures, I owe you for stepping in. I—"

Without warning, she yanked the hair on the back of his head, and rammed his face against the tank – cracking his nose. As he doubled over in pain and tremor, she kicked him solidly across the chest, then slugged him.

He staggered, dazed, and she tripped him fluidly by sweeping his ankles. Once down on his rear, she kicked his ribs, then lifted him by the shirt and backhanded him across the cheek.

She backed away, breathing hard and holding her aggravated wound tightly. "Your purpose is spent; now your life is forfeit. Remember that."

She walked away, and Tantalus now regretted deeply not having better aim.

* * *

Geist traversed past the immense hangar doors into the maw where the zeppelin was perched for quick repairs. Catwalks and scaffolding surrounded it, as airship technicians inspected the engines and outer shell while the equipment was brought in to refuel the reservoirs.

The Major-General glanced up, feeling significantly small beneath the imposing steely form of the zeppelin, but not in stature as Guderian descended the rungs to meet him.

The Colonel saluted, seeming particularly light in his steps. [Are we ready to begin mass production, Generalmajor?]

[The work's begun to transport the prototype to another factory by train, though with the loss of the papers, the schematics themselves will remain with the British engineer until he transcribes them, but ultimately the Kaiser waits his decision on you, Oberst. They call it the "Great War", but most of us would like to see it at an end, and in our favor.]

[Don't be upset about my tardiness,] Guderian casually reassured. [I was simply removing the unpredictable elements from our master stratagem.]

Geist had no qualms about putting this regular army colonel down a notch. [A reckless wager that costed us time and resource. Incinerating the old forest, ravaging a village – you're bloodthirsty.]

[Would it please you to know that the enemy agent had been captured by my hand?] Guderian had too much pride to be stepped on by a Landwehr militiaman, regardless of his rank.

[And if the Ottoman had his way when I last left him, then this 'friend of Melville' is dead.]

Geist was unimpressed. [A bold claim for something that you were not a witness to.]

[Don't test me, Generalmajor,] Guderian warned.

[Then don't take me for a second-rate officer, Oberst,] Geist rebuked in kind. [Make your official recommendation to the Kaiser, and be done with your duties here.]

Geist turned about face and strode away, leaving Guderian fuming with hurt pride.

One of the airship pilots approached. [Sir, the zeppelin will be flight-ready in six hours—]

Guderian viciously slapped the pilot across the cheek. [Did I give you permission to speak?! If this ship's not ready by the time I return, I will have you summarily executed!]

Guderian stormed away, scattering everyone else from his vindictive path.

Chapter 22

*T*he truck convoy, far slower than the zeppelin, passed the barricade of the armament factory grounds and entered the motor pool. The Landsturm assault troopers, sifting through their loot, were oblivious to the stowaway riding in one of the lagging truck's undercarriage. Holding tight to the support strut, and avoiding all contact to the wheels and the axle, Brazen kept his sight on what little he could see beyond the motorized belly of the heavy vehicle.

It jolted to a stop alongside the dozen others in the fenced lot, and its engine gears clanked shut. With shouts from the company officers, the soldiers disembarked, and assumed their station at the barracks a short distance away or attended to duties elsewhere in the facility.

The beating Brazen had received had taken its toll on his muscles and bones, and he longed to sleep soundly on a soft mattress, but his will to finish the job was much too potent. He held on to the strut, patient and attentive until all became quiet, then he carefully released himself from the undercarriage, and flattened his belly on the ground. There was no one in sight, but he stuck close to the shades.

He pulled out a bundle of dynamite from his gear, modified with an unusually long fuse, and lodged it to the vehicle's underside fuel tank. With the explosive secured using spare boot laces, seeming an appropriate device to enact a bit of vengeance on behalf of the dead villagers, he lit the fuse with a match.

He crawled out from beneath, and moved to a crouch – peering around again for spotters and stragglers. The trucks were parked less than twelve feet from each other, and he sprinted to the nearest one, moving from cover to cover until reaching a drainage hole.

Forcing the heavy iron lid open, he paused briefly as a familiar white and grey Fokker fighter took off from the airfield and flew overhead. The other Fokker monoplanes were still grounded, assigned to the zeppelin's keeping as it refueled and re-armed within the airship's colossal hangar.

Keeping his rifle slung over his shoulder, he scaled down the opening, making certain to close the lid after him, and landed inside the cramped storm drain with a splash of dirty water. He studied both directions for traps and obstructions with what little light streamed into the drainage, then purposefully entered murk toward the armament factory, which very much reminded him of those harrowing times leading up to the first day of the Battle of the Somme digging tunnels under the enemy machine gun nests with a volunteer team of expert sappers and miners-turned-soldiers. The musty smell of the scraped, chalky earthen walls, suffocating heat from lamps, and the sweat borne from toil and nerves, overwhelmed the senses. The silence was a godsend, for even a cough would alert the Germans, and so excavations were timed with artillery bombardments from either side at the risk of the tunnels collapsing atop of them.

The crowning moment, Brazen remembered as he rounded a junction in the storm drain, was planting the explosives in such great numbers directly beneath the German fortifications, that the explosion was heard from Lochnagar and Hawthorn Ridge to the outskirts of London. The macabre aftermath, and the crater that transformed the French landscape was a historic turning point in military tactics, and brought home a dose of trepidation to soldiers trapped in static trench warfare. Although he imagined the armchair commanders, detached from the blood and gore of the frontlines, were already staging a bigger and deadlier mine somewhere along the Western Line.

Several rays of faint light pierced the darkness, and he stood beneath the grated drainage cover leading to the main factory. Prying the lid aside, Brazen climbed out of the gutter onto the main factory's production floor. It was dark and empty of personnel, but the husks of future tanks were dimly revealed. He counted at least half a dozen waiting to be constructed, and knew he needed to sabotage Germany's efforts to build them.

He looked around for a means to set his plan to motion, and quietly inspected a group of oil barrels and equipment crates until he discovered what he needed.

Taking a crowbar, he pried open the lid one of the barrels, then kicked it over to let the flammable liquid spill all over the floor. He moved on to the next barrel....

Sitting comfortably on his robust Harley-Davidson Model 16F motorcycle, Geist sifted through Brazen's journal with keen interest, although perplexed by the text written in Japanese. Behind him, Tantalus, pouting with his nose bandaged tightly, worked alongside a group of artillery officers in preparing the tank's primary weapon test, while Colonel Guderian directed a professional photographer, loaned from the regular army, to take visual records for the Kaiser and the General Staff. The photographer used a folding strut Goerz Anschütz and a Zeiss Minimum Palmos folding plate hand camera to capture the best angles of the tank, and Guderian made certain nothing and no one else was in those frames save for himself.

Junigatsu kept a close eye on the British engineer, with a palpable chagrin between her and the turncoat, then strode over to the Major-General.

Tantalus glowered at her back, his bloodshot eyes filled of malice. But twisted thoughts gave way to ensuring his super-tank's offensive capabilities were on par with its impressive mobility.

"Tell me," Geist asked, sensing Junigatsu's approach, "what does this mean?" He showed her a part of the page in the journal that he was unable to translate, and she read it plainly.

"The samurai will fade. The world will change. The sword will always remain."

Geist pondered the meaning, though knowledgeable in many subjects, philosophy was not a subject he had time for. "Fascinating string of words..."

"The tank's ready for its weapon test, Generalmajor." Junigatsu was eager to take her unsanctioned copy of the tank blueprints, swiped before Brazen destroyed the rest of the designs, and return to home soil. "It's fully armed, and frankly, I don't trust him on the trigger."

Glancing at the tank, Geist was indifferent to her anxiousness, or the engineer's outlived usefulness. "Tantalus is a vain man, but few of us know how to operate that thing just yet. With all things considered, I have one of my best cannoneers with him, but you can join their company if it means peace of mind for us all."

Baron Justus piloted his white Fokker monoplane over the green landscape, unaccompanied by his squadron and in no particular hurry, following the main road to the small village where Guderian had captured the British operative. He scoured the area between the buildings, seeing nothing of interest until crossing over the village square. With the town square serving as a landmark, he circled around until he spotted a few saddled horses trundling about and grazing unsupervised, then saw the bodies of the cavalrymen sprawled dead near the well.

One of them, clear as day from his Turkish uniform, was Zag.

[What goes around, comes around,] Justus muttered, almost gladdened the Ottoman got his due, but overridden by the dire implications that the saboteur was still alive.

With all due haste, he pivoted the fighter around, and raced back to the factory grounds.

Chapter 23

A deafening explosion ripped apart the motor pool, inciting a pillar of fire and smoke that ejected the demolished truck a hundred feet in the air before it crashed sideways onto another vehicle and through the perimeter fencing.

The shockwave startled all of them, rattling windowpanes and shaking the ground, and after a confused pause, the air sirens wailed. Landsturm infantrymen poured from the barracks, believing they were under imminent aerial attack until the officers directed them to the blaze that threatened to ruin all the vehicles parked in the motor pool, and spread through the airfield and barracks.

Guderian shoved the photographer away to keep him from documenting the explosion, and searched the sky. [Are we under attack?!]

[Secure the tank, Oberst!] Geist commanded. [Escort it back to the factory!]

[Yes, Generalmajor!] With a sharp gesture for the squad to follow him, Guderian paced toward the tank. [Get it moving now!]

Tantalus, his anxiety surfacing, didn't wait for a translation to know what to do. He clambered down the hatch, followed by one of the artillery officers, and with a roar from the tank's engine, it crawled toward the safety of the factory.

Geist, unshaken by the rumble of the tank as it moved past him, strolled over to his motorcycle, and took the binoculars from its pouch. He scanned the wrecked motor pool, seeing soldiers scramble through the acrid smoke to control the fire.

Junigatsu looked on, her instincts surfacing. [It's him.]

The tank rolled into the secure confines of the gloomy production floor amidst the pre-natal husks of future tanks. The Landsturm troopers secured the premises quickly, and Guderian waited by the warehouse doors – basking in the light pouring in from outside. There was still no sign of hostile aircraft, but it was best to assume the worst.

[Seal the doors shut! Weld it if you have to!]

Two of the soldiers slung their rifles over their shoulders, and applied their weights into closing the two large doors. The beam of dusty light slowly shrank until it enveloped them into the relative gloom with a thunderous clang.

The hatch atop the tank swung open, and Tantalus stuck his head out nervously after the German cannoneer climbed out. He felt doubly claustrophobic being stuck in here with the Colonel and his goons.

"This better be a case of accidental incompetence," Tantalus reproached, failing to hide his anxiety.

Guderian had more pressing matters than to deal with the neurotic engineer. "Stay in that tank, Englishman," he warned with a heavy accent, then turned to the cannoneer. [Protect this machine at all cost, even if you have to kill that idiot.]

Tantalus grimaced at the rebuttal, and what sounded as a hazard to his health, but something nagged at the hairs on his neck. Some distinct smell in the air bothered his nose, and despite the low lighting from the electric lamps, the floor of the factory seemed to shimmer strangely as if waterlogged. Yet it was too slick to be water.

"That smell... is it petroleum?"

Guderian and the troopers now began to notice the oddities, including the sticks of dynamite lodged in the factory's support beams.

Guderian, for all his pride in his own military genius, felt dumbfounded. [Dynamite...?]

The flash and boom of a bullet split through the dimness, and killed the cannoneer – sending the man sprawling on the tank with a sickening thud.

Brazen emerged from the shadows, his Lee-Enfield rifle aimed and steadied, and one by one, he shot the troopers while keeping his pace balanced. Guderian, cornered between the stairwell and the factory doors, fell under the dead weight of one of his soldiers and lost his pistol in the process.

Brazen shifted his rifle to Tantalus, but the panicked engineer stumbled back inside the tank – closing the hatch shut. By then, Guderian had pried himself free of the body lying on top of him, and retreated to the upper catwalk, narrowly escaping the loss of his hand as Brazen's assault struck the metal stairwell with a spark. Seeing no other way out, the Colonel crashed through the upper level window, and fell nearly a dozen feet from the armament factory's second floor to the ground.

He landed hard with a roll onto his shoulder, glass shards raining around him, but despite his cuts and a fractured hip, he struggled to his feet and limped toward the barracks.

Letting the German officer go for now, Brazen strapped his rifle over his shoulder, circling halfway around the tank's front for a means to breach it. He stopped when he saw Tantalus' terrified eyes peering through the driver's narrow view-slit.

Brazen revealed a set of matches, lit it, and threw it under the tank. He turned his back and calmly strode away as the flame became an inferno. He exited through the same window as the Colonel, knowing the spilled petrol had leaked into the drainage. Unlike the haughty officer, he landed on the grass without effort.

Alone now, surrounded by the dead soldiers, the horror of being burned alive overwhelmed Tantalus as the fire enveloped the tank and spread throughout the factory, igniting the clipped fuses of the dynamite bundles scattered throughout the building. Shaking in uncontrollable fear, he screamed and cursed to no avail.

No one was coming to save him.

The explosion tore through the factory, foundering its roof and walls as the impact rattled through the ground a hundred yards in all directions. The skeletal framework collapsed in on itself, and subsequent inner explosions from leftover ammunition spit out flaming debris high into the air.

Brazen, his back to the destruction and pressed against the safety of the large train parts piled outside, secured the sheathed katana to his belt as his offensive stockpile dwindled. He looked ahead, where the Landsturm infantry now drew their entire attention toward him.

Guderian, his courage enforced with sheer numbers, fervently rallied the troops, and surrounded Brazen's position while overhead, the familiar propeller drone of the Baron's white Fokker rocketed across the sky.

The Baron was appalled by the devastation, the flames reflecting off his goggles. He had returned too late for the forewarning, but not for vindication. Circling around the rising smoke, he observed soldiers encroaching across the field in a crescent, their guns aiming at the culprit standing alone at the epicenter of the havoc.

The Major-General's motorcycle furrowed through the mass of soldiers, and so Justus delayed pulling the trigger for risk of incidentally mowing down his own people, and looped around to provide cover for the forces below.

The Landsturm infantrymen kept to their pace, driven by Guderian's leash, but allowed Brazen a wide berth. When Geist raced past them at the motorcycle's fullest throttle, with Junigatsu riding behind him, the soldiers hesitated – some redirecting their rifles' aim.

The motorcycle grounded to a stop before Brazen, uplifting dust under its wheels, and Geist waited for Junigatsu to get off, indifferent to her injury, before he shut the engine and rested the bike on its parking strut.

With the factory enraptured in a hellish inferno, Geist could no more feel its heat than the dark anger bubbling deep in his gut. He was given a simple command, one that netted large material rewards, as well as prestige, and he had failed. Was he to blame the incompetency of his officers? Or the poor quality of his troops and equipment? He was conceited enough to say his leadership was not in question, and that there was only one man to blame for this monumental disaster. He stared hard at Brazen, sizing him up for a quiet moment, then raised a white-knuckled fist to his soldiers behind him.

[Hold your positions!] Geist ordered sharply, trying hard to contain his frustration.

The soldiers halted their slow advance as the Major-General commanded, and Guderian, soured with pain as he was, wasn't about to contest the order. Safely behind the rows of his troops, the Colonel watched on with mixed fascination and spite.

Removing his riding goggles, Geist dismounted from the motorcycle, and stood to his full height. No one made a sound, and the air was filled with the crackling and spitting of the flames, and the buzzing of the Baron's monoplane.

Brazen remained cold and determined. It will take more bullets and blades than what he had left in his arsenal to extricate himself from this mess, and so he focused on the Landsturm's commander.

"Your duplicity is the stuff of myth," Geist praised in an attempt to verbally disarm his opponent. "Today you may have stalled progress, and you have shown me that we cannot win by sheer strength of arms alone. I can't help but admire what you've accomplished... Still, I cannot let you live."

Unbuttoning his coat, Geist pulled Brazen's journal out, and showed it to him. "I had a glimpse into your soul, and for the glory of the old days when disputes were settled with swords; I will grant you a parting gift."

Geist snappishly tossed the journal to Junigatsu, then unsheathed two long-bladed German bayonets from the motorcycle's side pouches. Their machete-like blades gleamed red from the fire.

Brazen was a little surprised, if not suspicious. The Major-General had the advantage and opportunity to end this quickly, but chose instead to test his fencing skills, perhaps as a show for his demoralized troops, or more likely for petty, close-quarters vendetta.

Brazen glanced at the soldiers surrounding them, then to Junigatsu, before resting his hard gaze on the tall Landwehr regiment commander. He unlatched the katana, loosened his posture while keeping the blade in its scabbard, and waited.

Geist attacked first, his long legs covering the distance as he chopped the air where Brazen had been a split second before. He thrusted and swung again, but Brazen exercised the best defense and avoided all attacks.

Unnerved, Geist wanted a fight not a dance. "Stop parrying and fight me!"

Moving with the speed of a demon, Geist unleashed the might of both bayonets on Brazen, but the latter continued to avoid what attacks he could, and blocked expertly with the lacquered scabbard against all else. One opportunity exposed Geist's head, and Brazen speared the butt of his scabbard up Geist's jaw.

Geist snapped back from the hit, disoriented for a heartbeat before humiliation spurred him again at Brazen.

Everyone else watched on anxiously, but Guderian alone saw it as an opportunity. He turned to the Landsturm captain beside him. [Instruct all troops to fire on my order.]

The Landsturm officer was taken aback. [But, sir, the Generalmajor is in the line of fire.]

Guderian was perfectly aware. [A tactical risk I'm more than willing to take. Ready weapons, Hauptmann.]

As the order was carried out, and the soldiers formed firing lines, the clash of swords and wits continued, until Geist's flurry of thrusts finally nicked Brazen's forearm.

Grimacing but keeping his composure, Brazen fluidly backed away, and pulled the broken katana from its scabbard. The blade gleamed with unparallel sharpness and rooted history – six inches of its pointed tip missing.

Geist grinned, his heart thumping with excitement. [At last.]

Brazen committed to the next assault, swinging high and reversing his scything actions to catch Geist off-guard. The Major-General backpedaled, not expecting such fierceness, and blocked weakly with both bayonets when the broken katana's edge skimmed too close.

Feigning an attack to Geist's ribs, Brazen reversed direction with a flick of his wrist and sliced at the side of the Major-General's leg. Brazen immediately assailed with his scabbard, knocking one of Geist's bayonets from his hand.

The German blade embedded itself in the ground, too far to retrieve, and Geist furiously clouted his other bayonet and ripped a gash across Brazen's chest – missing flesh, but cleanly tearing his shirt and jacket.

Both men moved away from each other for a momentary respite, the lost bayonet impaled between them, and the drone of a monoplane propeller suddenly filled the air. Out of the blue, Baron Justus strafed the field, throwing dirt and debris in the air as his Fokker's machine guns smashed a path toward Brazen.

The repeated gunfire missed, and the distinctive grey-white Fokker zipped past at low altitude then climbed back to the heavens.

The distraction gave Geist a boost forward, and he charged at Brazen at close range, all absolutism and determination channeled to his bayonet-sword.

Brazen avoided the blade and parried, but he was smacked unexpectedly by Geist's elbow. Adapting quickly to the roughneck tactics, and missing a kick to his knee, Brazen returned the favor by using the scabbard as an extension of his fist, and clobbered the Major-General across the temple and ear.

Geist snarled from the welt and ringing, as he twisted around and caught Brazen on the cheek with the tip of his bayonet.

As blood trickled down to his jaw, Brazen viciously stabbed the katana's broken tip through Geist's biceps.

Geist reacted instantly with a heel-kick to Brazen's abdomen, pushing him back far enough for Baron Justus to strafe his position again. The ground churned up as the silvery Fokker flew past, spurting a cloud of heavy dust between Brazen and Geist.

Expecting a dead man, Geist's eyes opened wide with surprise as Brazen sprinted forth like a hornet – pushing away the dust as he side-swung the open end of the scabbard. From the recess where the blade would slide in, the missing six-inch tip of the katana shot out, and impaled itself deep in Geist's chest.

Geist gasped, the air knocked from his lungs, and dropped to his side in shock.

The ground trembled as the charred skeletal remains of the factory imploded under waning flames, and Guderian gave the cue to his soldiers. [Fire at will! Kill him!]

At that moment, the Fenrir tank violently burst out of the blazing rubble with its sMG 08 machine gun firing. It treaded between the Landsturm ranks and Brazen at full speed, thrashing through the soldiers, and crushing them blindly. The soldiers' gunfire ricocheted off the tank's armor, missing both Brazen and their general.

Hard at the controls, drenched in sweat and his skin covered in blisters, Tantalus was lost in total madness as he fired at everything in his sights. The residual heat rising from the hot metal surfaces around him, the hellish clacking of pistons from the engine, and the stream of spent bullet shells clattering away from the machine gun's ammo feed spurred his recklessness.

The death of all who had tortured him, denied him, and abandoned him was his only consolation.

The Landsturm infantrymen scattered in panic, as many of their brethren were massacred by the tank's ferocious squall. When the machine gun quieted down with a whirring whine, the main cannon pivoted about and fired a volley into the mass.

The explosion threw bodies and chunks of earth several yards in all directions, and pounded the retreating survivors to the ground.

Guderian, his arm bleeding profusely after being pared by stray shrapnel, struggled back to his feet. His ears were ringing, his uniform torn and stained, and his sight was fuzzed as soldiers ran past him. Yet in the mayhem, he watched as Brazen quickly grabbed Junigatsu by the arm and yanked her out of harm's way, cradling in the tank's umbra beside the downed Major-General.

Using all his remaining strength, Guderian hobbled with haste toward the zeppelin hangar.

Chapter 24

*J*unigatsu pulled away from Brazen, still unwilling to trust him despite potentially saving her life a second time. She glanced at Walden Geist, who was writhing in pain on the ground, then up at the steaming tank as it started to sluggishly roll toward the airfield.

"Tantalus has lost it," she said. "He's trapped inside – both in the tank and his mind."

Brazen unkindly pinned Geist with his knee, and yanked out the six-inch blade tip from the Major-General's chest. Ignoring Geist's curses, he stood up and sheathed the katana while striding toward the motorcycle – which had fallen over to its side during the scuffle.

"You can wait around for something better to happen, or you can help me beat this thing." Brazen strapped the scabbard to his belt, lifted the motorcycle back on its wheels, and mounted it as the tank whirled around to face them.

Junigatsu hesitated, until the hollow of the tank's cannon bore directly at her. Tantalus' ire spared no one, least of all her, and she darted to join Brazen as he started up the engine.

They bolted away, and the tank turned around in fervent pursuit – firing its main cannon to gouge out a crater in their path.

Stiffening her jaw against every bump on the terrain that brought a jolt of pain to her tender side, Junigatsu wrapped her arms tightly around Brazen's chest as he steered the motorcycle with expert finesse around downed soldiers, cargo boxes, and managing the gaps between buildings. The tank, its armor tarnished by the fire, smashed through everything in its path – sending debris in all directions. Its machine gun opened up, puncturing round after round into the ground and building walls, careless of any troopers that strayed into the crossfire.

Brazen maneuvered the motorcycle into a narrow alley between two hangars. The tank swerved heavily to its left to pursue, one track locking in place while the other cycled rapidly to facilitate its ungraceful shift in course, and bore through the hangar's doors and out the back. Both motorcycle and tank slid sharply to their sides, changing the direction of their impetus at a near perfect right angle, and headed past the broken fencing into the burning motor pool.

Pistons and gears hissed and squealed as Tantalus continued to push the mechanical limits of the tank's power plant. His bloodshot sights were dead-on Brazen and Junigatsu, heedless of everything else, but somewhere in the back of his intellect, he reconciled on his innovative approach of the self-loading mechanisms he implemented for the machine gun and turret. These experiments he had kept secret, as a failsafe to his continued usefulness to men like

Geist and Guderian, but now it mattered less as the complex devices were splitting at the seams.

Angrily pulling back a lever, then ramming the device forth, he forced the next shell into the strained self-loader that fed the main cannon.

"I will crush you for what you are!" Tantalus yelled at his foes, his maniacal laugh echoing as he fired.

The tank's cannon jerked back, causing its forward momentum to teeter slightly from the recoil. The volley destroyed one of the parked trucks, catapulting troopers attempting to flee, and sent three other vehicles toppling onto their sides.

Brazen snaked from left to right, avoiding the back-blast, and pivoting past the earlier truck wreck that was used as a diversion. The tank rammed aside the ground vehicles with decreasing effectiveness, crushing everything under its tracks, scraping its underside and piling rubble to the tank's detriment. Small explosions set off as petrol canisters blew under extreme duress, further overwhelming the tank until it got stuck between clutters of debris.

With all momentum lost, the tank's powerful engine revved as its treads reversed direction to dislodge itself. Like a caged beast, it thrashed frenziedly, carving out the asphalt beneath it and sending jagged debris into the air.

Brazen slowed down, looking back at the machine with Junigatsu in the forlorn hope that it had finally broken down.

The tank turned placid, its tracks steaming, when it suddenly roared back to life – launching the tank from the twisted wrecks and back on the chase.

Brazen pulled back the throttle, and zoomed away as the tank fired its main cannon again – blasting a fissure in the airfield....

Holding on to the railing of the hangar's gangway, Guderian climbed up the rungs to the zeppelin's control car. The zeppelin pilots were in a frenzy to depart, especially with his arrival, even though the airship mechanics have long since abandoned their posts.

Explosions from outside the hangar reverberated throughout the facility, the cacophony getting louder and closer with each blast.

[Oberst!]

With a sidelong glance, Guderian saw a Landsturm officer carrying the battered Geist by the arm.

[You survived.]

Geist ignored the Colonel's bitterly astute observation. [We can still salvage this situation. With limited fuel and armaments, Tantalus will find himself at our mercy once more.]

[Fool, the damage is done,] Guderian spat out, abandoning respectful decorum reserved for ranking officers. [There's nothing else to do except to bombard this base, and deliver the pieces to Berlin.]

Had it not been for his wounds, Geist would have stood taller than the insolent Colonel. [I will not abandon my soldiers to your whims, Oberst.]

[Then die alongside them.]

Guderian pulled out his sidearm and shot the young officer propping the Major-General, then turned its muzzle to Geist and shot him thrice. Ignoring the shock of the pilots, he continued his defiant march onto the zeppelin.

Brazen hurried across the airfield, passing the crimson Fokker planes and their startled pilots amidst take-off preparations. Junigatsu risked a glance behind her as the tank crashed through one of the hangars, shearing the wings off the closest of the planes like a wrecking ball. The heavy machine gun shredded the airfield, killing some of the mechanics, and as the tank's tracks continued rolling, it bumped aside the parked Fokker planes, even with some pilots stranded in their cockpits, until its engine suddenly stalled.

Reaching the end of the runway leading to the zeppelin hangar, Brazen slid to a stop and got off.

"What are you doing?!" Junigatsu forced herself fully onto the motorcycle's saddle to keep the two-wheeled vehicle steady. "If we drive into the forest, he won't be able to follow!"

"Sounds as good a plan as any." He dropped his rifle, and pulled down the gear from his back.

Junigatsu took control of the motorcycle's handlebars, as the tank's powerful engine sputtered.

"Now's our chance, Brazen, please!"

Brazen turned to her, holding her so intimately that she saw the copper speckles rimming his brown irises. There was something about this woman that spoke to his soul, proving that he still had one. He knew she was a foreign agent whose goals were to deliver advanced tactical plans to an Empire on the verge of reviving its samurai traditions of brutal war and conquest, potentially becoming a dangerous superpower within the next two decades. Despite this, against his own indoctrination, he had entrusted her his journal, and a piece of the life he had lived thus far.

[You're my only way out,] he said in her dialect. [Go.]

There was something deep in his words, and without time to fathom them, she sat back on the motorcycle's saddle and rode away.

Tantalus punched the instrumentation panel, cursing and yelling as steam hissed from fractured pipes around him. The fumes strangled him, and irritated his eyes, but the physical nuisances were suppressed by utter psychosis.

"Wake Fenrir, *wake!*" he screamed, seeing Brazen through the view-slit. "Kill them! Kill them before they get away!"

The *Fenrir* reanimated with a shrill and knell, ever livider than before, and dragged itself out of the crushed planes lodged beneath its tracks.

Brazen faced the mechanical beast, pulling the last of the dynamite from his gear, then tossed the bag beside his rifle. As the tank gathered speed, gunning straight at him, the rumbling reverberated profoundly beneath his feet. Brazen stood his ground, and lit the short fuse.

The machine gun assailed the path before the tank, until the last bullet was spent, yet the *Fenrir* continued its monstrous impetus. Brazen waited as the seconds passed, then at the last possible moment, he leapt aside while tossing the dynamite between its tracks.

The explosion blew apart the road and idler wheels, loosening the track plates, and the powerful snapping force flipped the tank laterally end over end until it smashed through the side of the zeppelin hangar.

The zeppelin itself was spared the consternation as it lifted away from its berth, and out into the open, following the exodus of the airship mechanics and fire crew from the damaged building.

From the control car's viewport, Guderian and the zeppelin crew were stunned by the terrible collision, seeing the mess unfurling well below them, and the bedlam spreading throughout the airfield.

A lone figure knelt tiredly amongst the carnage.

[Once we're clear,] Guderian said to the pilots, [prepare to launch everything we have on the enemy's position.]

Chapter 25

On a knee and breathing hard, Brazen looked up at the portentous German airship as it gracefully pulled back from its berth. Being close enough to the ground, he distinguished the Colonel inside the control car amongst his pilots and gunners.

Flying above them, the Baron's pale Fokker circled anxiously for a clear shot. The ace pilot had been witness to the destruction below him, and was unable to prevent the loss of men and materiel to such unrecoverable degree. He now itched for payback.

Brazen was exhausted, his bones and muscles told him so, but he soldiered on, tiredly reaching for his gear to pull out three rifle grenades he had appropriated from Captain Goodwin's armory before leaving the trenches – each with a steel rod threaded to its base – then lifted himself up using the Lee-Enfield rifle as leverage.

He unlocked the bolt-action rifle's ammo cartridge from its socket, and replaced it with a ballistic cartridge from his jacket pocket. Quietly asking the angels above to lend him some strength, he ambled toward the zeppelin, calmly inserting the first grenade into the rifle's barrel.

Holding the other two grenades like spare arrows in his trigger hand, he carefully aimed at the airship's framework.

He fired.

The projectile discharged out farther than a man could throw, covering over three hundred meters before it exploded against the zeppelin' forward section.

The zeppelin shook violently with a terrible undulating noise, startling Guderian and the pilots. The light of the flames wavered threateningly before them as it washed over the nose of the large craft.

[We're clear of the hangar!] Guderian directed with impunity. [Climb higher into the air, you dolts!]

Historically, since the inception of airships in wartime, it took lightning bolts in rough weather, poor maintenance, and full squadrons of determined fighters to bring down a German zeppelin. A single soldier stood no chance.

[Climb! Climb!]

Preparing the second rifle grenade, Brazen shot again. The blast pitched the zeppelin's lower tailfin, nearly capsizing the airship in mid-air. Small flaming breaches across the outer foil that contained the gas bladders burned away at its protective shell. The gunners, normally courageous enough to ride the winds while holding on to their platform-mounted gun nests, leaped from the zeppelin altogether, risking a fatal drop to the factory fields below.

The grey-white patterned Fokker monoplane swept about in an attempt to cover the zeppelin. The Fokker's guns wildly pelted the ground around Brazen to little effect.

Brazen unleashed his last rifle grenade at the zeppelin's control car itself. It frayed the Maybach engine strutted at the car's side, and the propeller blades carved through the zeppelin's belly. The control car's supports crumbled, bracing wires snapped, and the keel tumbled toward to the ground. The zeppelin's outer covering was consumed by runaway fires from within, and losing all levity, crashed onto the tarmac.

A backdraft of fire and ash enveloped Baron Justus' fighter as it passed through it – unable to avoid it for the enormity of the fiery vortex. The monoplane's engine choked, and Justus was forced to land. The fighter bounced on its wheels, gliding across the grass, but the wings kept stable, and landed safely.

Brazen immediately dropped the rifle, and sprinted toward the Fokker. He pulled out Cyrus' Colt .45 from its holster, fluidly climbed atop the wing, and quickly approached the cockpit. He pressed the gun against the Baron's chest – who was still disoriented from the emergency landing – and fired at point-blank.

After giving his all to this last act, Brazen let go a long outbreath, and wearily climbed back down to the ground. He glanced up at the sky for a brief respite, for Cyrus' memory, then returned the Colt to its holster, and leaned back heavily on the Fokker.

His mission was done. The war still raged on.

To his pleasant surprise, Junigatsu returned on the motorcycle, stopping a few feet before him. She shut off the overheated engine, divided in her feelings for this man. She wanted to say something, but held back and let the silence fill the air.

The stillness would not last.

From the zeppelin hangar, the tank emerged, hurling aside sheared struts and scaffolding from its dented armor. Brazen stood fully to face it, between it and Junigatsu, having nothing left to defend himself except his sword.

Its cannon was bent, and its machine gun was gone. The treads were noisily sliding apart from the bent road wheels until it parted off completely; the internal gears grinded against each other, slowing the bulk down, until the entire machine died a few meters from Brazen.

Brazen unsheathed the broken katana, and with tremendous effort, climbed onto the tank just as its hatch wobbled apart from its hinge. Sigmund Tantalus, his head cracked open and bleeding, crawled out. His mouth was agape, salivating in delirium.

"... the wolf..." he mumbled between shallow breaths. "Odin's bane... my bane... my—"

All life drained from Tantalus, and he died atop his tank – halfway out of its hatch. His blood seeped from too many wounds, covering the riveted armor plates in red.

Brazen lowered his sword, knowing for certain that victory was his.

Chapter 26

Amongst a beautiful garden with thriving flora and stone pathways following a gentle stream, Junigatsu waited patiently for her host to arrive. Dressed in her kimono, she felt strangely out of place after arriving in home shores only a few days before, after years apart, yet there was comfort to be found here.

She held with her a small package tied together with golden lace.

In the shadow of a Sakura tree, she discovered funerary stone tablets marking the graves of family members long since passed. One seemed more recent than the others, perhaps by a decade or two, and was inscribed by a non-Japanese name.

Clearing the simple gravestone of fallen leaves, she assumed it was Brazen's mother. Stepping back, she honored the dead with a bow.

Escorted by her two daughters, Lady Minori arrived, and Junigatsu bowed to her respectfully.

[Rarely do we get visitors from the Kempetai,] Lady Minori greeted politely, [but you are welcome to my family's house.]

[Thank you, my Lady, but I'm here on behalf of your adopted son.] Junigatsu unraveled the package, and humbly handed

Brazen's journal to the stately woman. [He asked me to deliver this to you, his cherished memories, and with all his love.]

The elderly lady, overwhelmed with emotion, grasped the journal to her bosom and shed tears. Junigatsu felt her own heart twist with feeling at the good deed she had done. The war brought nothing but the worst in people, and she was glad she was able find her way out of that darkness.

[Thank you,] Minori said, and bowed to her guest. [You told my daughters he had saved you twice over, yet in so many ways, you had saved him. This here is a promise that he will return.]

Surrounded by blossoms, Junigatsu smiled warmly. Deep down she knew the geopolitical landscape was changed irreparably. This war, when it ends, would set into motion a great many ambitions bound to collide.

The world outside the trenches will not be so welcoming to the soldiers who fought and bled for its freedom.

Chapter 27

With the day faltering over the horizon, and a malicious thunderstorm brewing, German soldiers were retreating from their forward positions, carrying what equipment and supplies they were able to muster in short notice, and abandoning their posts before the Allied artillery descended upon them.

Officers cried out orders, directing their units out of the trenches and out of the enemy's wrath. Despite the discipline and training of the soldiers, the sheer desperation created havoc and confusion, causing many dissenters to surrender to the Allied forces en masse.

Amongst those officers trying to infuse order in the ranks was Franz Lieder, eager to escape out of the trenches himself. He directed a pair of soldiers toward the last of the ammo caches.

[Hurry up and carry that to the wagons!]

The soldiers complied promptly and dragged the cache out of the trench with them. A mortar exploded overhead, lighting the countryside briefly, and showing no one else in the trench with Franz.

He looked around nervously, rubbing his knuckles to keep them warm from the evening chill. He pulled up the collar and lapel of his trench coat, as another explosion sparked above the trenches, not realizing Brazen was prowling behind him.

[Instead of home,] Franz thought quietly to himself, [I think I'll lay low in Paris...]

Brazen swiftly cupped his hand over Franz windpipe, and pulled the German double agent close to whisper in his ear. "Your war's lost, and the next one will have no use for you."

Brazen speared the broken katana through Lieder's back, piercing spine and heart and killing him instantly. He pulled out the sword, letting go of Franz Lieder's lifeless body and left him in the ditch.

Wiping the blood off the blade, Brazen returned the katana to its sheath, and climbed out of the trench. Framed by the last wisps of sunset, with lightning flashing within the dark clouds, he tossed the German helmet aside, and walked toward the victorious Allied front.

Manufactured by Amazon.ca
Bolton, ON

42004877R00106